RINK OF DREAMS

RINK OF DREAMS

NANCY L. M. RUSSELL

KEY PORTER BOOKS

Library and Archives Canada Cataloguing in Publication

Russell, Nancy L. M. (Nancy Leigh Mary), 1963–
     Rink of dreams / Nancy Russell.

ISBN 978-1-55263-935-1 (pbk.)

I. Title.

PS8585.U774R55 2005   jC813'.54   C2005-902728-2

The Canada Council for the Arts | Le Conseil des Arts du Canada since 1957 | depuis 1957

ONTARIO ARTS COUNCIL
CONSEIL DES ARTS DE L'ONTARIO

The publisher gratefully acknowledges the support of the Canada Council for the Arts and the Ontario Arts Council for its publishing program. We acknowledge the support of the Government of Ontario through the Ontario Media Development Corporation's Ontario Book Initiative.

We acknowledge the financial support of the Government of Canada through the Book Publishing Industry Development Program (BPIDP) for our publishing activities.

Key Porter Books Limited
Six Adelaide Street East, Tenth Floor
Toronto, Ontario
Canada M5C 1H6

www.keyporter.com

Text design: Ingrid Paulson
Electronic formatting: Jean Lightfoot Peters

Printed and bound in Canada

07 08 09 10 11   5 4 3 2 1

THE SNOW DOGS ARE COMING

SOMETHING BIG WAS about to happen. Gary knew it as soon as he saw the television trucks parked outside the Charlottetown Civic Centre.

"Oh, I know," said Todd, smiling as he reached into the trunk of his mom's car to grab his gear. "They must be here to watch our practice." The boys mumbled a quick goodbye to Mrs. Manning. Then they slung their hockey bags over their shoulders and hurried toward the rink.

Like Todd, Gary had had his equipment ready for days, just waiting for this moment to arrive. His first practice with the bantam AAA team! As he pushed open the door to the arena, Gary couldn't help but feel the butterflies in his stomach. Making the AAA team was important, even though it was only his first year moving up from peewee. Soon, there would be scouts at the games and talk of junior hockey or even the ultimate dream—a career in the NHL. A year in AA could put a stop to all that. It would be nothing short of a disaster. And Gary wasn't about to let that happen, even if the second-year bantam players were older and bigger.

Gary hated to admit it, but size was something he thought about a lot. Both he and Todd were in Grade 8, but Gary was still half a head shorter than his best friend. Todd had dark hair and brown eyes, and it seemed to Gary that the girls were always chasing after him. Compared to Todd, Gary thought he looked like a little kid; his unruly blonde hair and baby-blue eyes were bad enough, but the freckles—left over from a summer spent outside—were almost more than he could take.

As Gary entered the arena, his jitters about bantam were quickly forgotten. Just inside the doors, a crush of people and cameras had gathered. The boys squirmed their way around the edge of the crowd. A podium and speakers stood in the middle of the commotion. "Ladies and gentlemen, we're going to get things underway now," a man in a navy blue suit and tie announced, as he signalled the crowd to quiet down. "I know that some of you are on deadline and so we'll get through our announcement as quickly as possible. First, I'd like to introduce Clark Dinsmore, president of the New Mexico Snow Dogs hockey team."

Gary and Todd looked at each other in surprise. What was someone from the Snow Dogs doing here?

"Thanks for being here today," Clark Dinsmore began. Although Dinsmore towered above the podium, Gary still had to crane his neck to see him above all the cameras. Dinsmore was a former NHL player and his face bore the scars of his rough-and-tumble career. He wore a jacket and turtleneck and Gary thought he looked every bit the hockey executive. "We're pleased to announce that Charlottetown is the new home of the Snow Dogs farm team."

Gary turned and whispered to Todd, "The Snow Dogs play in Cape Breton. What is he talking about?" There was a mur-

mur from the crowd, along with a flurry of flashes from the photographers. Several reporters shouted questions at Dinsmore, but he raised his hands to silence them.

"We have a lot of work to do," he said. "The American Hockey League season begins in two weeks, and we only finalized the arrangements with the city earlier today, so we're going to be playing catch-up with the other teams. The players will arrive over the next couple of days and we'll begin practising for our first exhibition game, which is just ten days away."

"Why did you pull out of Cape Breton?" a reporter shouted.

Gary noticed that Dinsmore looked slightly annoyed at the question. He paused, as if choosing his words carefully. "We had a year-to-year deal with the folks there and we were not able to reach an agreement for this season. We were approached by the fine people of the city of Charlottetown and we decided that this was the perfect home for the club."

Before the reporters could ask any more questions, Dinsmore motioned for the mayor to join him on the podium. Dinsmore grabbed a Snow Dogs jersey and turned, smiling, to the cameras. Graham Williams, the somewhat plump, grey-haired mayor of Charlottetown, posed with the sweater. Gary giggled and elbowed Todd as the mayor struggled to pull the jersey over his suit. Finally, Williams handed the keys of the city to the former NHLer.

"This is a big day for Charlottetown," said Mayor Williams. "We welcome the Snow Dogs to our city. We promise them the support of the people of Charlottetown—some of the greatest hockey fans in Canada."

A cheer went up from the crowd. Gary jumped as he suddenly felt a hand on his shoulder. He turned and looked up into the face of Coach Vince Mulligan. "You boys coming to practice?" Mulligan hissed.

Mulligan wore the jacket of the legendary Charlottetown Abbies, the most winning hockey club on the Island. He had been the bantam AAA coach as long as anyone could remember and many of his players had gone on to play junior hockey in Ontario and even to be drafted into the NHL. Mulligan worked his players hard. But as he told anyone who asked, the results spoke for themselves.

Gary and Todd picked up their hockey bags and followed their coach back through the crowd. Gary took one last glance at the scene in the lobby, wishing he could stay. After all, this was the biggest news ever to hit Charlottetown.

"Couldn't we just stay until they're finished?" he pleaded with Coach Mulligan, who was now striding purposefully toward the dressing room.

"You've wasted enough time with that nonsense," Mulligan responded coldly, ushering the boys through the door.

"It's not nonsense," Gary argued. "This is a big deal. An NHL farm team is coming to Charlottetown. I've been waiting all my life for this!"

The Coach rolled his eyes. "Why? Do you think the scouts are finally going to discover ya? Please. You boys should concentrate more on your skating and shooting and a whole lot less on your daydreaming. Now get a move on!"

Gary watched his coach storm out of the change room. He quickly threw on his hockey gear and decided against arguing any further. Coach Mulligan was in one bad mood, and Gary couldn't think of anything to say that would make a difference. Still, as he and Todd stepped on the ice, Gary wondered why the Coach was so irritated by the news about the Snow Dogs.

Coach Mulligan stood near centre ice with a whistle in one hand and a hockey stick in the other. He was a short man, even on skates, but still bulky with muscle. He was thought to be in his late fifties, and his thinning black hair was giving way to a shiny dome, hidden today underneath an Abbies ballcap. Mulligan had played several seasons in the big leagues, back in the days when there were only six teams in the NHL. His word was gospel in hockey circles around town.

Mulligan was trying to put the boys through a passing drill. But this afternoon, everyone was having trouble concentrating. The cameras had moved into the rink area, and Clark Dinsmore was standing at the glass, watching the boys practise. The cameras were still recording his every move.

"Look," whispered Todd, nudging Gary in the side. "Dinsmore's checking out our practice!"

"It's just for the cameras," Gary mumbled back. He watched as Dinsmore positioned himself so that all the photographers got a good angle.

"Manning, are you listening to me?" Coach Mulligan bellowed in Todd's direction. "It's your turn. Get moving!"

Gary snuck another glance over at the Snow Dogs executive. He was busy shaking hands with some of the city councillors who had been at the press conference. At the same time, the arena crew were scrambling around, putting up Snow Dogs logos. This was so cool! Before long, big-league players would be practising on the very same ice surface as him!

The sound of the puck sliding across the ice toward him shook Gary out of his daydream. He quickly took the pass and headed down the wing toward the net. This was no time to be caught looking. Sure, he'd made it through the first round of tryouts, which was more than could be said for some of the other peewees, but a spot on the team was far from guaranteed.

Gary's birthday wasn't until December, which meant that he was almost three years younger than the oldest player on the ice. In peewee, he had started to feel he was falling behind in size. Now, however, things were different. As much as he hated to admit it, Gary was uncomfortable for the first time in his hockey career.

A FEW WEEKS EARLIER, with his first bantam tryout looming in the distance, Gary had tried to talk to his dad. Ever since his father had given him his first stick and puck, hockey had been something special between them. Even his sister, Maggie, was part of it. Maggie had been playing hockey since she started school—she'd never bothered with figure skating or ringette. She was always eager to play pickup with Gary and his friends, and Gary had to admit, however grudgingly, that his sister was pretty good.

Every winter, the MacDonalds spent hours every evening, first planning and then preparing their backyard rink. Even on the coldest, most blustery nights, Gary, Maggie and their dad would be out carefully spraying the water on the skating surface, building layer after layer of pristine, smooth ice. When they were finally finished, the informal practices began. The boards surrounding the ice echoed every evening with the *whack-thud, whack-thud* of Gary's puck and the *scritch-scritch* of Maggie's blades slicing white lines across the glistening ice.

Over the years, the MacDonald rink became legendary. It had grown in size until it took over the entire backyard, and Gary's dad had even added netting around the sides, to keep the pucks in. He invented a homemade Zamboni of sorts, out of an old barrel, and put up several strings of lights. On many nights, Gary and Maggie stayed outside until their mom finally called them in for bed.

"I'm not sure I'm going to like bantam," Gary had said tentatively, as his father stared ahead at the television.

"You'll be fine," came the mumbled response.

"But the guys are a lot bigger than me," Gary persisted. This time, his father didn't answer at all.

"I wish you were going to coach again this year," Gary added, making one final attempt to get his father talking. Donny MacDonald was well known in Island hockey circles. He had been captain of the UPEI hockey team when they had won the university championship many years ago. He was still in great shape and had coached Gary every year since he had started organized hockey. Every year, that is, until this year. Since Gary's mother moved out, everything had changed. Donny was still handsome, with thick brown hair, peppered with hints of grey. But these days, Gary noticed his dad had trouble keeping his clothes ironed, and the house was always a mess.

Still no response. Gary sighed. He wanted to tell his dad about the bigger players that were likely to make the team—guys like Justin Johnston and Mike Bartlett. They were in Grade 9, a year ahead of Gary and Todd. These guys had deep voices and lots of facial hair. Many of them had spent the summer working out in the gym. They walked around the dressing room wearing only towels, flexing their muscles for everyone to see. The younger boys pretended not to notice, but Gary knew it was going to be rough. After all, these guys were on their team. What was going to happen when they faced the competition—with guys the same size or even bigger?

And, same team or not, Justin Johnston was going to be a problem. It seemed to Gary that Justin had been picking on him since novice. Gary always felt relieved when the older boy would move up an age group, leaving Gary and Todd to become the team leaders. A year later, though, they'd be reunited, and Johnston would seem to get even more enjoyment out of tormenting him. Gary tried to take comfort in the fact that his skills were as good if not better than Justin's, but that didn't always help, especially when he found himself face down on the ice after a brutal check.

Gary cringed as he thought about another year with Justin Johnston on his team. He really needed his dad's advice—not just about Justin, but about everything! But Donny MacDonald didn't seem in the mood to talk about Justin or about hockey. These days, he wasn't in the mood to talk about anything. Gary went upstairs to do his homework.

"How's it going?" Maggie called out as he walked past her room. Maggie was seated on her bed, surrounded by a pile of papers and books. She was sixteen, and in Grade 11 at the local high school. She had the same blonde hair as Gary, but hers was shoulder length and curly. She was tall and fit, thanks to all her time on the ice. While hockey was her favourite pastime, Maggie loved all sports, and she and Gary could sit and watch the sports channel for hours at a time, arguing about their favourite teams.

"Okay," Gary shrugged. "I guess I'm getting a bit freaked about the tryouts. I know the guys trying out this year. Some of them are way bigger than me, and kind of rough."

His sister raised her eyebrows. "What do you mean rough?"

"They just seem to want to hit everything in sight, you know," Gary explained. "I mean, I know checking is part of the game. But even in peewee they had their elbows up and were always pushing and shoving."

"It's gonna be tough on a shrimp like you!" she teased.

Gary glared at his sister. "I could skate circles around your wimpy team. You couldn't hit the broad side of a barn, never mind the net."

"Okay, okay," Maggie waved her hands in surrender. "Obviously I hit a nerve. Any luck convincing Dad to coach?"

Gary shook his head. "He just sits there in front of the TV every night. He didn't even want to talk about it. I thought he'd make a big deal out of this year. You know, being bantam and all."

"He *is* being weird," Maggie agreed. "I mean, I know it sucks that Mom moved out, but I am *so* sick of everyone dwelling on it."

Gary bristled at his sister's words. It had been six months since Martha MacDonald had sat down with Maggie and Gary to tell them she was moving into her own place. The family had had several meetings with a counsellor, and at the end of it, he and Maggie were told that they would stay with their dad. They could visit their mother on weekends. Gary was still angry that his mom hadn't offered either of them a chance to come live with her. He'd never stayed over at his mom's place, even though she asked him every week.

"I don't blame Dad," Gary replied in a testy tone. "It's great that Mom's life is going so well, but she really didn't give him much of a choice, did she? She kind of sprang this on us."

"I think they stayed together for years just so we wouldn't get upset," Maggie replied. "And if they're weren't happy, then why shouldn't they split up? Everybody does it."

"Yeah, sure," Gary muttered, heading for the door. "None of my friends have screwed-up families."

"Oh, grow up, Gary!" his sister snapped. Immediately, she looked like she regretted her words. "Let me know when you have your schedule for the season. I want to check out your team."

"I have to make the team first," Gary replied.

"You will!"

Gary wasn't so sure.

NOW, A FEW TRYOUTS LATER, Gary watched Todd skate effortlessly into the corner, chasing down the opposing forward and slipping the puck away. Gary noticed that Todd was almost as big as the older players.

Todd headed back up the boards, ready to pass him the puck for his turn in the drill. Suddenly, Gary went flying as Justin Johnston hit him with a whopping bodycheck.

"MacDonald!" Coach Mulligan yelled, "Get on yer feet. You've got to take the hit and get right back up. This isn't pee-wee anymore."

Gary slowly got to his feet, his elbow throbbing with pain. He looked around for the puck and discovered that the drill was over. The players were already gathering at centre ice.

"Are you okay?" Todd whispered as Gary skated over, carefully readjusting his elbow pads.

"I banged my elbow," Gary grimaced, rubbing it carefully. He'd have a huge bruise by this time tomorrow.

"Welcome to bantam, ya wuss," Justin sneered. "You may have been a star in peewee, MacWuss, but you're playing with the big boys now."

"That's right, MacWuss," Justin's buddy, Mike Bartlett, snickered. "Good one, J-Man. MacWuss. That's going to stick."

The two boys skated away to talk with some of the other older guys. They pointed at Gary and laughed.

Gary stared straight ahead, pretending he didn't see them. Half an hour later, Coach Mulligan blew his whistle and once again called the boys to centre ice. They were all still getting to know Coach Mulligan, but his temper was legendary. As Gary looked at the expression on Mulligan's face, he could tell that the players were about to see that temper first-hand.

"A few weeks ago, there was some pretty big news around here," the Coach began, in a hushed voice. "And I know that there are TV cameras here every day and big-league hockey players hanging around, and that you're all headed straight to the NHL."

The two assistant coaches seemed to sense what was coming. They quickly skated over to the boards and started picking up the pucks. The Zamboni driver waited patiently at the edge of the glass. "Yes, the Snow Dogs are in Charlottetown. And yes, that *is* big news. But when you are on the ice, *your minds are on this team.* The Charlottetown Abbies Bantam AAA. *Do I make myself clear?*"

By the time he delivered the last sentence of his speech, Mulligan was screaming at the top of his lungs. His face was bright red and his baseball cap had almost popped right off. Usually, Gary would have been tempted to laugh, but he could tell that the Coach was serious. Gary nodded earnestly and noticed that all his teammates were doing the same. As they skated off the ice, Gary was surprised to see his father waiting by the glass. He gave his dad a quick wave and went to get changed.

Donny MacDonald was waiting for his son outside the dressing room. Gary's heart sank when he saw his father talking to the Coach. "Now I'm in for it," he muttered under his breath.

"The offer stands," Coach Mulligan was saying. Gary looked at his father, trying to read his expression. What offer?

"Thanks, Vince, but I've got my hands full at home now," Donny replied. Gary noticed that his dad suddenly seemed flustered. Donny quickly changed the subject. "Looks like you've got a good group. You should do well."

"Lots of young kids, though," Mulligan shook his head. "Could go either way with lots of 'em."

"Yeah, bantam's tough," Donny agreed. "Separates the men from the boys, doesn't it?"

Suddenly, a camera crew went rushing past, almost knocking Gary into the wall. Coach Mulligan chomped on his cigar and spat in their direction. "What a load of bull that is," he said tersely. "As if the Snow Dogs are going to stick around here for long."

Donny tried to lighten the mood. "Maybe it will be good for the boys to see some real talent up close."

"It just puts all kinds of foolish ideas in their heads," the Coach muttered and headed back into the dressing room.

"Why does the Coach have such a beef with the Snow Dogs?" Gary asked his dad as they made their way to their minivan.

"It's a long story," his father said, throwing Gary's gear into the back.

"Is it because he once played in the NHL?" Gary persisted.

His father sighed. "He had a good career, Vince did. You know, it was tough to even make the League back then. Just six teams. His brother played for a bit, too. You know, Socky?"

Gary looked at his dad with surprise. Everyone in town knew Jamie Mulligan. He worked at the Civic Centre, driving the Zamboni and cleaning up the stands. He walked with a limp. People called him by his nickname, Socky, because he wore thick woollen socks all year round.

"I didn't know Socky played in the NHL," Gary said.

"It wasn't for long. Early in his first season there was an accident. He was slammed into the boards and broke his foot in six places. That was his last game."

"Couldn't they just give him a cast? Why didn't he play again?" Gary asked.

"That's the part that still infuriates Vince. The team didn't want to pick up the medical costs. So they cut him. He came home, almost broke. By then, the foot had set wrong. They broke it again and reset it, but it was never the same. Vince says it hurts so bad he can hardly even put on a skate."

"That's why he wears the big socks," Gary exclaimed and his father nodded.

"Vince wanted to hire a lawyer and sue the team, but the league would have blacklisted him. Socky made him promise not to pursue it, but Vince has been sour on the NHL ever since."

LATER, AT THE SUPPER TABLE, Gary and Maggie watched yet another news report about the Snow Dogs.

"Some of the girls in my class are going to the practice on Saturday to check out the guys," Maggie grumbled. "Here I am, trying to be taken seriously as a hockey player and all they want to do is date a future star. I could just puke!"

"What's the big attraction?" her father asked, as he passed the pizza box across the table to his daughter.

"Dad, get a grip. These guys are stars, right? What do you think the attraction is?" Maggie snorted. "I mean, these are girls who think the junior Abbies are impressive. Obviously, they have no taste whatsoever."

"That *is* gross," Gary nodded. "And besides, how many of these guys will actually make it to the NHL?"

Donny shrugged. "It depends. The way the league keeps adding teams, they seem to take almost anyone these days. But realistically, probably only a handful will make it. And if they were real superstars, they would have gone straight from junior to the National League. Maggie, I think your friends are out of luck," he smiled at his daughter.

"They're *not* my friends," Maggie protested, then changed the subject. "Why did the team come here, anyway? Charlottetown isn't exactly big time."

"They were desperate," Donny explained. "They couldn't make a go of it in Cape Breton, and they needed to move somewhere fast. I guess we offered them the best deal."

All three fell silent as Clark Dinsmore appeared on the television. Gary strained to catch a glimpse of himself and Todd on the ice behind him, but the cameras were only focused on the president of the team.

"I hope the people of Charlottetown will come out and support the Snow Dogs. We're looking forward to a long and winning career here," Dinsmore concluded.

"Our firm is getting a couple of season tickets," Donny told Gary and Maggie enthusiastically. Then his face grew glum. "But the games are usually on the weekend, and I'm sure you'd rather go with your mother anyway."

Donny went to the fridge and grabbed a beer. He left his half-eaten slice of pizza on the counter and went to the living room.

"Why doesn't he just stop talking about her?" Maggie muttered, staring angrily at the TV. "Dwelling on it isn't going to make anyone feel better."

"She started it by leaving," Gary replied. "He just wanted to take us to the games. That's all he said."

As he walked past the living room, where his dad had turned on the other television, Gary wished there was something he could say, some way he could break through his father's silence. He wanted to tell him that he was angry too, that he wanted things back the way they used to be. But there was something about the expression on his father's face that made Gary think there was no point in even trying to talk to him now.

Gary went to the back door and grabbed his hockey stick and a ball. He spent the next hour on the driveway, pounding the ball against the side of the house, practising his slapshot. In his mind, Justin Johnston was in net, and he aimed the ball right at the goalie's head. His elbow throbbed, but Gary didn't mind. Anything was better than going back in the house.

THE FIRST PRACTICE 2

GARY ARRIVED AT THE Civic Centre bright and early Saturday morning. The Snow Dogs were scheduled to practise at eleven, but by eight o'clock, there were already people milling around. Socky Mulligan was hobbling up and down the stands, picking up loose candy wrappers and empty paper cups. He was whistling cheerily to himself, keeping a close eye on the action below. Gary looked around anxiously but his coach was nowhere in sight. He settled into a seat above the door to the Snow Dogs' locker room. Perfect—the ideal vantage point from which to watch the arrival of Charlottetown's newest celebrities.

The first person Gary recognized was the farm team's head coach, Dave Anderson. He was a bulky redhead, with a buzz cut that made him look even tougher. Anderson was wearing a wind suit with the Snow Dogs' logo on it, and he already had his whistle around his neck, even though practice was still hours away. The newspapers said that Anderson had played in the minor leagues himself, only making it to the NHL for three games. Now, however, Anderson had a new goal: to make it to the big leagues as a coach. The outcome would depend on how well his young players performed.

"It's a crapshoot," Anderson had told a reporter from the *Guardian*. "You don't know how these kids are going to do. They all want to make it to the NHL. Some of them resent being down here in the minors. Others look at it as a challenge."

Gary wondered how the players were feeling now, about to skate in Charlottetown for the first time. Some were just moving up from junior. Others were older—career minor leaguers who were still hanging in, hoping for a big break. A couple of the Snow Dogs, the lucky ones, were still with the "big club," at the NHL training camp. They would be the last cuts from the NHL team and would only arrive in Charlottetown days before the season began.

"Finding everything you need, Gunner?" Anderson's booming voice rose up into the stands from the tunnel leading to the team's dressing room. Gary looked down and saw the Coach talking to an older man that Gary didn't recognize. "Gunner" was also wearing the red, white, and black Snow Dogs track suit and a matching baseball cap. Wild grey hair stuck out on all sides, and he looked like he needed a shave. He was wearing thick glasses.

"I've got the skate sharpener all set up and I'm starting to work on the sticks, eh," Gunner replied.

Anderson slapped the old man on the back. "I don't know how I would've made it through last year without ya, buddy. You let me know if there's anything at all that you need."

"How're the boys looking?" Gunner asked the Coach, nodding his head toward the ice surface.

"Hard to tell," Anderson replied. "Depends who they decide to keep and who gets sent down. I've heard good things about this new goalie, Lambert. Sanders is back, so we're solid on the blue line. And I'm hoping to get Laroche back, but he won the league scoring championship last season and he deserves a crack in the bigs."

"He'll be in a foul mood if he doesn't make it again this year," Gunner mumbled, picking up an armful of sticks as the Coach disappeared into the dressing room.

The old trainer looked up and noticed Gary sitting in the stands. "Keep yer paws off the sticks," he snapped. "And no autographs today, kid." Gary was too surprised to say a word. Talk about rude!

"As if I'd want one from any of these guys," he muttered to himself.

"Gunner!" A tall man in sunglasses and a leather jacket grabbed the old trainer in a bear hug. Gary leaned over the railing to catch a glimpse. Darby Sanders! Sanders was one of the best-known of the minor-league Snow Dogs and he'd gotten lots of media coverage when the team was in Cape Breton. A rugged thirty-year-old who often led the league in penalty minutes, Darby was the Snow Dogs' captain, and the backbone of the team's defence. He was the kind of player that fans loved to watch, and Gary suspected he'd be very popular in Charlottetown.

"What, they're letting an old geezer like you play again this year?" Gunner joked, pushing Sanders away with a grin.

"Speaking of geezers, can I carry some of these sticks for you, old man?" Sanders teased in return.

"How are Jennie and the kids?" Gunner asked.

"Great," Sanders answered, picking up his bag of gear. "Her family's in Moncton, so we're happy to be closer to home."

Sanders took a look at the rink and walked out from under the balcony to peer up at the stands. For a moment, his eyes met Gary's and Sanders gave a gentle smile.

"The ice looks good, and the barn's a fair size," Sanders said to the trainer.

"Yeah, but don't bother unpacking your bags," another voice replied. A tall blonde player appeared in the locker room doorway.

"Quit your whinin', Duffy," Sanders gave his teammate a playful punch in the arm. "It's just like you to look on the dark side."

"Hey, Cape Breton, Charlottetown, it's all the same to me," Duffy answered, folding up his expensive sunglasses and tucking them in his pocket. "I just wish it was New Mexico."

"I feel bad for those fans back in Cape Breton," Sanders continued. "Now they'll never get the championship."

"And who knows how long we'll be here," Duffy replied.

"Get off it," Sanders answered. "They can't keep moving us every year."

"Oh, no? Just wait until the next big arena gets built in the States. I hear there are a couple in the works already down south somewhere. My brother's playing in the Texas league and he says they're all talking about getting AHL teams. If they come calling, you don't think the owners will jump?"

Sanders shrugged and the two players disappeared into the dressing room.

As the players continued to trickle into the arena, Gary noticed a couple of high school girls hanging around at ice level, giggling to one another. He rolled his eyes. A couple of young boys holding Snow Dogs banners were also there, but none had the nerve to ask any of the players for an auto-graph. Or maybe they just didn't know yet who these guys were. Gary only knew a handful of their names himself. Some of them looked not much older than the junior Abbies, who also played at the Civic Centre.

Gary had always dreamed of moving up to play with the Abbies in the Maritime Junior Hockey League. And watching the Snow Dog players arrive at the rink, his dream didn't seem so impossible after all. They were just regular guys, not like the superstars that he saw on TV.

By eleven o'clock, quite a crowd had gathered around the boards. There was even a smattering of applause as the play-ers poured out of the dressing room and onto the ice. Last out was Coach Anderson, who gathered the players together at centre ice. A series of drills quickly began, with a goalie at either end. Gary recognized many of the drills—dumping the puck and chasing, passing, shooting, two-on-ones, one-on-ones—but, man, were these guys fast!

It may have been the same ice surface, but the Snow Dogs covered it a lot faster than Gary and his teammates. They hit hard, too, especially for the first practice. Gary rubbed his elbow, remembering his own checking accident. Justin Johnston's taunt rang in his ears. Watching the older players, Gary made a promise to himself: he would work harder to get bigger and stronger, just like the pros.

After practice, the players exited the dressing room, their hair still wet from the shower. Finally, two of the young boys who'd been holding the signs worked up the courage to ask for some autographs. Most of the players stopped and signed their names quickly, but Rob Duffy just rushed by the boys, pulling on his dark glasses as he headed toward the arena door.

"Sorry, kids, not today," he sneered, without even a glance in the boys' direction.

"Duffy!" a voice bellowed. Coach Anderson appeared in the corridor beneath Gary's seat. The player froze in his tracks.

"A word," the Coach said, waving Duffy over. Gary couldn't see Duffy from where he was sitting, but he could just barely hear the conversation.

"What was that?" Anderson snapped.

"What? The autograph thing?" Duffy blustered. "Hey, that was a joke."

"Listen, you twerp. I put up with your attitude all last season and I'm sick and tired of it. You may think you are a star, but take it from me, you're not. That's why you're still here. So until you smarten up and get your butt in gear, this is where you're staying and you'd better learn to like it. And that includes being nice to the people who live here. Got it?" The Coach's voice got louder and louder as he bawled out the young player.

"Okay, okay," Duffy muttered, heading over to where the young kids were standing. He snatched their pieces of paper and quickly signed his name, glaring over at the Coach as he did it.

What a jerk, Gary thought, getting up to leave. Looking down into the corridor, he saw Coach Mulligan walking toward the rink with Russ, one of his assistants. Gary quickly ducked back into his seat.

"When are we going to make the final cuts?" Russ asked. Both men stepped to the side, making way for the Zamboni. Mulligan waved to his brother, perched high on the ice machine.

"I'll give them all a few more practices," the Coach answered. "There are just a few I can't decide on. Like the MacDonald kid. I mean, he's Donny's son and all, but I'm not sure he's big enough to take it."

"I feel bad for the kid," Russ replied, lowering his voice. Gary's face flushed with anger and embarrassment, and he leaned over the railing, straining to make out their words. He just had to hear what the Coach had to say.

"What do you mean?" Mulligan asked.

"I hear Donny and Martha are having some problems. I don't know for sure, but word is she left him. Happened over the summer," Russ explained. "Apparently Donny's taking it hard; the kid, too."

"Damn shame," the Coach replied, as the two men disappeared down the hallway. "But I don't want that kid getting hurt. If he's not ready, he's not ready."

Gary slammed up his seat and stormed toward the door. How could they talk about his parents like that? It was none of their business! Then it dawned on him. Coach Mulligan was thinking of cutting him! Gary had always played AAA. He had been the top scorer last year in peewee and runner-up for league MVP—he was a shoo-in to make the Abbies bantam AAA team. Or so he'd thought.

Gary was too busy fuming to watch where he was going. He stepped out of the arena and into the parking lot just as a Jeep careened around the corner. The driver slammed on the brakes, almost knocking Gary over.

"Hey, kid, look where you're going!" One of the players stuck his head over the top of the Jeep and waved a fist in Gary's direction. Gary glared right back. "Bunch of hicks." The player spoke to his companion, but in a voice deliberately loud enough for Gary to hear. The Jeep pulled out of the lot, screeching its tires.

Gary leaned against a wall of the Civic Centre, trying to catch his breath. A steady stream of vehicles was pouring out of the parking lot onto the street. Practically all of the players drove bright, expensive vehicles. Several had loud music playing, and they all pulled quickly out of the parking lot, paying little attention to the traffic beyond. When the lot had finally cleared, Gary made his way back into the arena to call his dad. He really needed to talk.

Maggie answered the phone. "Where's Dad? I need to talk to him," Gary sputtered. There was a silence on the other end.

"I don't think you want to talk to him right now," his sister whispered. Gary could tell by her voice that something was wrong.

"What's going on?"

"I'll tell you later, okay?" his sister insisted.

"Look, Maggie, I just heard Coach Mulligan say that I might be cut, so I need to talk to Dad. Okay? Are you happy now?" Gary shouted. He looked around the empty lobby of the arena. Thankfully, no one appeared to be listening.

"I'll be there as soon as I can." Maggie hung up the phone before he could reply.

Gary went back outside and threw himself down on the lawn, absent-mindedly plucking at the blades of grass. What was going on now? This was so typical. Here he was, really needing his dad, and he was nowhere to be found.

His thoughts turned back to Coach Mulligan's words. Gary shook his head, as if to erase the memory. It didn't matter. He *was* going to make the AAA team, no matter what. He would start lifting weights and would practise even more. Maybe he and his dad could even get started on their backyard rink. There were lots of chores to be done in the fall, before the cold weather began. It might even make his dad feel better.

Ever since Gary had started playing in an indoor arena, he hadn't had as much time for the backyard rink. This year, however, he'd found himself thinking about it a lot. Maybe it was his age. At thirteen, he knew he was facing the most important year yet of his young hockey career. It was do or die for him and his teammates, and given the pressure he was under, Gary wasn't surprised that The Dream had returned.

It had started many years ago, when the rink was first built. In The Dream, the MacDonald rink sprawled to fill the backyard—which was suddenly large enough to host the final game of the NHL playoffs. Burly speedsters whipped up and down the length of the ice and when Gary looked closely, he saw that they were the biggest stars of the game. And he was there, too, skating along with them, his treasured number 87 emblazoned on his jersey. The Dream always ended the same way—with Gary scoring the winning goal to claim the hallowed Stanley Cup.

It was only a dream. But on the backyard rink, Gary always knew that anything was possible. And yet this year—this really important year—Donny MacDonald hadn't even started to prepare the yard. Usually by now, he'd have Gary and Maggie raking up leaves to make room for the boards, which needed to go down before the cold weather arrived. Gary looked forward to this ritual every year, certain that the rink was the secret to his success so far. Now, he needed it more than ever.

Just then, the MacDonalds' minivan pulled up alongside the curb. Gary climbed in and looked at his sister. "What's going on?" Gary asked softly.

"It's Mom. Dad ran into her downtown and she was with some guy. Holding hands. Dad's just sitting in the living room, drinking one beer after another. I didn't want him to drive."

Gary stared at his sister, confused. "Who's the guy? Did you know about this?"

Maggie shrugged. "She kind of hinted she was going on a date a couple of weekends ago. I just pretended not to hear and she didn't say anything else. I didn't want to make it into a big deal. And I know you're still mad at her so I wasn't about to tell you!"

"I *am* mad and it *is* a big deal!" Gary snapped. "Don't you get it? This is *all* a big deal. For Dad *and* for me. I don't get why it isn't a bigger deal for you."

Maggie winced and Gary instantly regretted his words. He stared out the window as the minivan turned on to their street and into the driveway. For a minute or two, nobody moved. They just sat there, staring at their house.

"I miss her too," Maggie said finally.

"Then why do you always act like nothing's wrong?" Gary asked, in a softer voice now.

"It's easier, I guess," Maggie replied. "I want Mom to be happy. I want Dad to be happy, too. I can't change what happened, and it hurts too much to think about how things used to be."

"Do you really think they hated each other all these years?"

"No," Maggie answered. "I just think Mom changed. Remember when she went back to school? She was like a kid again. And then when she got the job at Rutherford's she was really proud. I think she just felt different about things. Not better or worse. Just different."

Gary looked out at the living room window, wondering what his father was feeling. "What's going to happen to Dad?"

"He'll get over it eventually. And maybe he'll find someone else, too," his sister replied. "Hey—you didn't tell me about practice. What's going on with the Coach?"

Gary's heart sank. Just for a moment, he had actually forgotten about what Coach Mulligan had said.

"It's no big deal," he muttered, opening the door and heading to the back of the van to grab his hockey bag. He didn't want his sister to see the tears welling up in his eyes.

Gary went straight to his room and threw himself on his bed. He could hear his father pacing back and forth in the living room. Gary spent the rest of the evening staring at the wall, drifting in and out of a troubled sleep. The backyard rink was forgotten.

3 MAKING THE TEAM

THE NEXT COUPLE OF DAYS were a blur for Gary. His father walked around the house in a daze and not much was said by anyone. At practice, Gary tried hard to put the events at home behind him and to concentrate on impressing Coach Mulligan. But no matter what he did, things continued to go wrong.

"MacDonald, keep your head up when you take a check!"

"MacDonald, you're ducking away! Take the check!"

"MacDonald, get back up and skating. We don't have all day!"

Gary was starting to doubt whether he really wanted to make the AAA team after all. Coach Mulligan was constantly on his case! He grumbled about it to Todd after practice one day, but his friend didn't see the problem.

"Hey, at least he knows you exist," Todd muttered.

"That's surprising, seeing as I'm so small compared to the rest of you," Gary replied sarcastically.

"I thought you spent the summer lifting weights," Todd teased.

Gary flexed his arms. "Not that you can tell. It's easy for you. You just keep growing. I'm stuck the way I am, no matter how much I run or lift. I can't even gain weight, even though all we eat at my house is pizza."

"You'll grow, Gary, don't worry about it," Todd reassured his friend.

"And if I don't? That's the end of my hockey career."

"Well, I may be bigger, but that doesn't mean I'm going to make the team," Todd lamented.

Todd and Gary had been best friends since Grade 1. Since then, they'd played hockey together every winter, and soccer every summer. Gary was a frequent guest at the Mannings' Lakeside cottage and they'd had each other on speed dial since Grade 3. Todd was the more easygoing of the pair, always trying to get Gary to lighten up. Gary, on the other hand, was constantly marvelling at Todd's ability to breeze through life. He could get the phone number of the most popular girl at school without even trying. For his part, Todd was amazed by Gary's ability to get straight As without breaking a sweat.

When it came to hockey, the two friends were evenly matched. Todd had the edge in size, Gary in skill. But this year, it was different. To Gary, it felt like time was running out. If he was going to make the AAA team, he had to do something soon. Otherwise, Coach Mulligan was going to cut him, no matter who his dad was. At Wednesday's early morning practice, Gary decided it was time to really make an impression.

The team was divided into red and black jerseys. Todd ended up on the black team, while Gary donned a red jersey.

"I've got to do some checking," Gary muttered to his friend during the first break in play. "I've got to prove that I can do it."

"Lighten up, will you? You're going to make the team," Todd mumbled back. Gary glared over at Justin who was busy pushing around one of the smaller players. Justin would be the perfect target for his plan.

When the scrimmage started again, Gary watched for his chance. He skated around the edges of the action, hardly noticing the play. There was only one thing on his mind: showing everyone—especially Coach Mulligan—that he was ready for bantam.

The black jerseys got the puck and Justin and Todd headed toward the red zone, where Gary and another player were on defence. Gary had just lined up Justin for the check when Todd zipped in between them. It was too late to stop: Gary threw his full force into the check. His elbow caught Todd right in the stomach, knocking the wind out of him, and he fell hard to the ice. He landed awkwardly on his side and immediately started moaning in pain.

Gary dropped to the ice next to his friend. From somewhere across the arena, he heard Coach Mulligan blow the whistle.

"What the heck was that?" Todd gasped, holding his shoulder and writhing in pain. "Were you trying to kill me or something?"

"It was just a check. I didn't mean to wind you," Gary apologized. He reached out his hand to help Todd get up.

"Don't touch him," yelled Russ. The assistant coach skated over quickly and examined Todd.

"It's my arm," Todd whispered through clenched teeth. "I didn't get a chance to break my fall. I wasn't expecting the hit."

"I think it's broken," Russ told Coach Mulligan, who had also skated over from centre ice. "We'd better get him to the hospital."

Gary watched in horror as the assistant coaches helped Todd off the ice, still wearing his gear. Mulligan blew his whistle and gathered the team together at the boards. "Manning will be okay," he said, his voice calm and reassuring, and very different from his usual on-ice bellowing. "I've seen this before a hundred times. He'll be back in six to eight weeks, good as new."

Gary's heart sank. Six to eight weeks? Todd was going to be furious.

"I hope this shows you all the importance of checking right," the Coach continued, his voice returning to its normal pitch. "If you don't, you can hurt someone or yourself. I don't want any of my boys causing deliberate injuries to other players. That's not what the Abbies are all about." Mulligan looked around, making eye contact with each and every one of his players. Finally, he gave his head a slight shake and glanced at his watch. "Now go on and get out of here. We'll have the final lineup in place by next practice." Mulligan concluded.

"Nice going, MacWuss," Justin snickered as the boys skated off the ice.

"Great check," added Mike. "I'm sure Manning will appreciate your putting an end to his hockey season."

"It's too bad." Justin continued. "He was the only one of you peewee twerps who was going to make it."

"Six to eight weeks is not the whole season, you nimrod," Gary snapped back. "Oh, I forgot. Counting's hard for you, isn't it?"

Justin grabbed Gary's jersey and started to push him toward the boards, but Mulligan's whistle put a stop to the fight before it started. Justin quickly dropped Gary's jersey and skated away, with Mike trailing behind.

"What was that all about?" asked the Coach.

"He said I had ended Todd's season," Gary replied. He had to try really hard to keep his voice from shaking.

The Coach motioned for Gary to follow him off the ice and into an empty dressing room.

"What was that all about? You were gunning for Johnston, weren't you?" Mulligan's voice softened slightly.

"I was trying to check," Gary explained. "I know you think I'm too small for bantam and I wanted to prove you wrong."

The Coach tried to hide his smile by chomping on the cigar that he'd pulled out of his pocket. "You know, Gary, I'm not exactly a giant myself. There's room in hockey for the big men and there's a place for skill players, too. I think that's where you should try to fit in."

Mulligan paused for a moment. "I'll keep you on the team for now. With Manning out, I'm going to need your scoring touch."

Despite everything that had happened, Gary couldn't help but smile. But Mulligan's face remained serious. "But listen, kid. If I think you're getting pushed around too much, I will send you down to AA."

Gary's heart sank, and the smile disappeared from his face.

"I can do it, you know," Gary protested. "I was the top scorer in peewee." The Coach put up his hands. Gary knew he'd said more than enough.

"It's for your own protection," Mulligan said with a tone of finality. "You're in for now. That should be enough. And don't tell anyone about our chat until I announce the team on Friday. Now head for the showers."

Mulligan walked out of the dressing room before Gary could say another word.

GARY COULD BARELY KEEP the news to himself. He'd made the team—the AAA Abbies—and he wanted to run through the school hallways shouting it out for everyone to hear. But the Coach had sworn him to silence. At least he'd be able to tell his dad and Maggie tonight. He sat in class, staring out the window with a contented smile on his face, not hearing a word the teacher was saying. Suddenly, the door opened and Todd appeared, his arm in a sling. Gary's eyes met Todd's and his friend turned away.

"Oh, Todd! What happened to you?" Ms. Chang asked, taking the note that Todd held in his good hand.

"Uh, a, uh, an accident at practice," Todd mumbled.

"How long will you have to wear the sling?"

"A week in the sling and then a week of physio," Todd replied. Gary noticed that everyone in the class was listening carefully.

"I'll be back with the team by the middle of November," Todd continued. "They thought it was broken. But it's just a bad sprain."

Todd looked over at Gary then and gave him a reassuring wink.

"What team is this?" Ms. Chang continued.

"The bantam triple-A Abbies," Todd replied. Ms. Chang looked impressed. Everyone in class was straining for a look at Todd's arm. Gary sank into his chair and pretended to flip through his textbook.

At lunch, Gary walked toward the cafeteria with a sense of dread building in his stomach. The Abbies always sat together at the long table in the corner, but how was he going to face his teammates today? When Gary walked in, everyone looked up, then quickly looked away. Gary took the hint. He stood, tray in hand, and looked around the room for an empty seat. He was turning to leave when he felt an arm on his shoulder.

"Where are you going?" Todd asked. "Come on and sit with the guys."

"I didn't think you wanted to talk to me right now," Gary replied, sneaking a glance at Todd's sling. Todd looked down, too, and just for a minute, a look of disappointment crossed over his face. He quickly shook it off.

"Hey, it was an accident, right?"

"Yeah," Gary responded. "It was Justin Johnston's arm I wanted to break."

Todd's sling was the main topic of conversation at the table, and Gary was happy to see his friend basking in the extra attention. He just hoped Todd's good mood would continue once the novelty of the sling wore off. And as much as Gary wanted to tell his best friend about making the team, he wasn't sure that Todd would be too thrilled to hear the news. Besides, Gary thought morosely, the Coach had been crystal clear about one thing: he could still be sent down to AA at any time.

Gary tried hard not to think about the Abbies for the rest of the afternoon. After Social Studies, he and Todd walked together to their lockers. It seemed to Gary that everyone they passed was pointing at Todd's sling. He could feel his cheeks flush with embarrassment. He swung open his locker door, almost slamming it onto Todd's arm.

Todd grinned. "Okay, okay. Once was enough!"

"Sorry," Gary said sheepishly.

Todd took a quick look around to make sure no one was listening.

"How's your dad doing?" he asked quietly.

"Okay, I guess," Gary said, reaching into his locker. He didn't want Todd to see the expression on his face—an expression that surely looked as miserable as he felt every time he thought about his parents. "He still isn't saying much. But it will be fine."

"Did you talk to your mom yet?" Todd inquired tentatively.

"Nah," Gary replied. "If she's got some new guy, I'm sure she's too busy to talk to me. I mean, she's got this new life now, right?"

"So you're not going to talk to her, *ever*?"

"Why bother? It's none of my business. I'm more worried about my dad," Gary said defensively. Todd dropped the subject.

FINALLY, THIS HORRIBLE day was over! As Gary walked toward the bus, hockey bag slung over his shoulder, he thought about Todd's arm, and about how their morning practice seemed a million light-years away. Had it really only been that morning? "Gary!" Someone was calling his name. "Gary!" He stopped and looked around. It was his mother, standing next to a car he'd never seen before—a shiny red VW Passat. She waved him over.

"What's with the car?" Gary asked, trying to hide his surprise. His mother reached out to hug him and then pulled back, as if she'd changed her mind.

"Climb in," she said, with a forced brightness. "I'm taking you to supper."

"I should phone Da...I mean, Maggie," Gary suggested, watching nervously as the big yellow school buses pulled past. He tried to duck behind the car. It seemed like everyone was staring at him and his mom. No doubt the word that his parents had split up was all over school. This would just add to the gossip.

"I've already talked to Maggie," his mother assured him. "She'll tell your dad."

Still, Gary hesitated. He felt strangely awkward as he stood there, staring at his mother in front of her brand new car—as if seeing her in another light. His mom *did* look different. She was still short and slim, with the same curly blonde hair as always, but Gary noticed she was wearing more makeup and a nice suit. An expensive briefcase was tossed in the back seat, and a state-of-the art cellphone rested on the console. A handheld organizer stuck out of her purse. And then there was that weird air of confidence about her—almost like excitement—that had never been there before.

"You don't have practice tonight, do you?" his mother asked, pointing to the bag slung over his shoulder.

"Uh, no, this morning," he muttered. Another bus pulled past and Todd hung out the window, waving his bandaged arm at Gary.

"What happened to Todd's arm?"

"It's a long story," he mumbled, getting into the passenger seat and slamming the door. His mother sighed and climbed in.

"Is pizza okay?" she suggested, trying to sound enthusiastic.

Gary groaned. "That's all we've been eating." Then he felt guilty, as if he had somehow betrayed his dad.

"How about burgers then?" Martha pointed the car toward downtown Charlottetown.

"Yeah, whatever." Gary stared out the window. No one said a word on the drive to the restaurant. Only when they were settled and had placed their order did his mom finally break the silence.

"Gary, I know you're probably mad at me right now, but I hope you'll help make this work," she began, fiddling with her fork and knife. Gary kept his eyes on the table. He felt slightly sick to his stomach and wondered if he would even be able to eat his burger and fries when they came.

"You should really come by to see my apartment. It's got a great view of the water," she continued. "Maggie really likes it there. And you'd have your own room." His mom paused. "How's it going at the house?"

"Fine, considering what you did," Gary blurted out. A hurt look passed over his mother's face, but it didn't stop him from continuing. "How's Dad supposed to feel? How are *any* of us supposed to feel?"

Tears welled up in his mother's eyes and Gary was suddenly embarrassed. He thought about getting up from the table and running but he seemed to be frozen in his chair.

"This isn't about your dad, or about you, or Maggie," his mother whispered. "It's about me. I just need to find out who I am. After all these years of being a wife and a mother, I need some time for me."

"So then why the boyfriend?" Gary snapped.

"He's just a friend," his mom replied. "I'm sorry we ran into your father…"

"I don't want to hear about it!" Gary got up and bolted to the bathroom. He ran into one of the stalls and slumped against the wall. He wanted to bang his fists against it as hard as he could. Instead he just stood there, trying to catch his breath. When he returned to the table, he noticed that his mother had paid the bill and asked for the food to go. He walked silently past her and out the door to the car.

"When does hockey start?" his mother asked, as she pulled out of the restaurant parking lot.

"I don't want to talk about it," Gary whispered. The rest of the drive passed in silence. In the driveway, Gary noticed his mother look nervously up at the house. She leaned toward him to give him a kiss, and he pulled away slightly. She recoiled quickly, as if she had been burned.

For the second time that night, Gary felt bad—ashamed of his own behaviour. He wanted to apologize for what he had said, but he couldn't make the words come out. Instead he muttered a quick "thanks for picking me up from school." His mother looked grateful, as if she realized he was making a peace offering.

Now it was his turn to look up at the house. He felt stupid, talking to his mother outside their family home. He wondered if any of the neighbours were watching, or—even worse—his father.

"Give me a call sometime," his mother said awkwardly, handing him the bag of food from the restaurant. "And I hope you'll come over some weekend with Maggie. Even just for supper."

Gary got out of the car and watched his mother drive away.

All of a sudden, the whole thing seemed real. His parents were actually splitting up. Up until now, it had been like his mom was away on a prolonged business trip. Now he realized she might be gone for good. He looked up at the house again and was startled to see his father standing on the doorstep. He looked tired, and defeated.

"Nice car," he said, a tone of bitterness in his voice. Then he turned and walked back into the house.

4 ARRIVAL OF THE SNOW DOGS

GARY SPENT A RESTLESS NIGHT, his mind filled with images of his parents and their separate unhappiness. He toyed with outrageous plans to get them back together but rejected them all. At four in the morning, he was still awake, fighting back tears, and picturing his family the way it used to be.

He must have finally dozed off, because the next thing he knew, Maggie was pounding on his door, telling him he was late for school. By the time he got downstairs, both his father and Maggie were gone. He walked to the refrigerator and opened the door. As usual, there was no milk or bread. Was he the only one interested in keeping the household going?

"Forget this," Gary snarled, slamming the fridge door. He looked up at the clock. If he hurried, he would just make it to his first class. Then he had a better idea. He was going to take the day off school. It was Friday, after all. Besides, he didn't want to see everyone at school looking at him like a freak. He was sure that his mother's new car and his parents' problems were the talk of the school today.

Gary knew just where he wanted to spend the day. He jumped on his bike and headed down to the Civic Centre. The arena was already buzzing with activity. There were a few people lined up at the box office as Gary walked past on his way to the stands. He stopped to look at one of the hundreds of Charlottetown Snow Dogs posters plastered all over the arena.

"Oh, yeah," he muttered to himself, scanning the poster. "It's opening night. Cool."

Tonight marked the official start of the season, and Gary remembered reading in the newspaper that there were special festivities planned for the game. There would be a pipe band and some speeches. Best of all, Clark Dinsmore was bringing some of his former NHL buddies to town to drop the puck. Gary had hoped that he and his dad would be coming to the first game, but his father hadn't said anything and Gary had been too upset after his visit with his mother to ask. His dad didn't seem very interested in anything these days, never mind a hockey game. Still, it was the sort of thing they used to do together. Not anymore.

Gary walked through the wide hallway under the stands. A stack of programs for the opening game was propped against one wall. Gary glanced around. No one was looking. Usually he would have felt guilty about taking something that didn't belong to him, but today he was in such a bad mood that he didn't even care if he got caught. He grabbed one and stuffed it into his pocket. Gary made his way to the same chair where he'd sat for the opening practice. He glanced up at the time clock on the wall. It was only 9:30. Still an hour and a half until the Snow Dogs' practice. Better than English class, though.

"Hey, kid, scram. This is a closed practice." It was Gunner, the old trainer, shouting at Gary from beneath the stands. The last time Gunner had yelled at him, he'd caught Gary by surprise. This time, he was ready.

"I don't want any autographs," he said as politely as possible. "I'm just here to watch. My team practises here, too."

The trainer's wrinkled face seemed to soften. "Isn't this a school day?" he asked Gary, trying to sound gruff.

"I, uh, just went to the dentist. So my mom and dad said I could have the rest of the day off." Gary was amazed at how easily he had lied. He cringed slightly at the mention of his parents, and then, to his embarrassment, he felt his eyes welling up with tears. He quickly wiped them away and hoped the trainer hadn't seen.

The old trainer squinted his eyes at Gary. He looked as if he wanted to ask more, but instead he picked up a pile of sticks and waved them in Gary's direction.

"Listen, kid, I can't let you watch practice. But if you've got some time, I could use a hand with these sticks," Gunner suggested.

Gary sprang from his seat. The program fell from his lap. He gave the trainer a guilty look, but the old man pretended not to see the stolen magazine.

Gary spent the rest of the morning following Gunner around. He listened carefully to the trainer's instructions and did exactly as he was told. He barely noticed the stream of players coming and going out of the locker room until Darby Sanders stopped by the trainer's room for a new stick.

"Who's the kid, Gun? Another one of your slaves? Get away from this guy, kid. He'll work ya to the bone," Darby teased the trainer, tapping Gunner playfully on the baseball cap with his stick. Gunner waved him away.

"Don't listen to him, Gary," Gunner replied in a loud voice. "Mr. Sanders is almost as old and creaky as I am. Every time I watch him play, I consider making a comeback myself." Darby Sanders left the room laughing.

"Why is the practice closed today?" Gary asked as the last players filed out of the dressing room and out onto the ice.

"It's to help get them into the game up here," Gunner said, tapping his head. "Coach wants them to feel that there's something special happening today. Get 'em fired up, ya know."

"I'd be excited about the game no matter what. It's opening night!" Gary replied.

Gunner shook his head sadly. "Ah, the enthusiasm of youth. Most of these guys lost it long ago. For them, this is a job. Just a job."

"But they could make the NHL! This is their big chance!"

"For some of them, yes. For others, that door is already closed. This is the next best thing, but in a way their dreams are dead. And that hurts."

Gary looked at the old man, hunched over the skate-sharpening machine. His tongue was pressed tightly between his lips as he gently massaged the skates over the blade of the sharpener. The flying sparks danced around the crazy grey hair that stuck out from Gunner's cap.

"You played in the NHL, didn't you?" Gary asked quietly.

"Just for a season," Gunner answered. A small smile danced across his face for a moment. "I wasn't superstar material, you could say. But I had one good season and then I hung up my skates. I've stayed in the business, though. All my life has been hockey."

Gary wanted to ask Gunner more about his time in the big leagues, but the trainer kept him too busy to talk. Before Gary knew it, the players were returning to the dressing room after practice.

"Thanks for your help, Gary," Gunner said, kindly but firmly. Gary realized that was his way of saying it was time to go. "Come by again when you've got some spare time. I can always use an extra set of hands."

Gary was almost out the door when Gunner called after him. "And Gary?" Gary stopped, hoping he wasn't going to get in trouble for stealing the program. "I hope your teeth are feeling better," the old trainer said with a wink.

GARY COULDN'T WAIT until Todd got home from school. He had to tell him about his day with the Snow Dogs! He grabbed his old stick and a tennis ball and practised his shot against the side wall of his house, waiting for his friend to come over. Todd looked worried as he jumped off his bike, grimacing slightly as he banged his bandaged arm on the handlebar. "What are you doing?" he asked, walking up the driveway. "Why weren't you at school today?"

Gary shrugged. "Didn't feel like it. I didn't miss any tests or anything. No one's going to care."

"Your mom and dad were at school today," Todd told his friend. Suddenly, Gary felt sick to his stomach. He stopped hitting the ball and stared at Todd blankly.

"I guess Mr. Bernard called them in when you didn't show up," Todd continued. "They didn't look too happy."

Gary sat down on the side door step, his adventures at the Civic Centre forgotten. What were his parents going to say?

"I was going to ask if you wanted to go to the Snow Dogs' game tonight but I'm guessing you won't be allowed to go," Todd concluded, going over to pick up his bike. "My dad gave me two tickets from his work. I guess I'll go with him instead."

"No, I'll go," Gary interjected. "What are my parents going to do? I just missed one dumb day of school. It's all their fault anyway."

"Why is it my fault?" Gary's father appeared from around the corner of the house. Todd jumped on his bike and rode off down the street, giving his friend a short wave with his sling. Gary felt a pang of guilt as he saw his friend wince with pain.

"I'll call you about tonight," Gary shouted after Todd. He glared at his father, daring him to pick a fight.

His father sat down beside him on the step. He was still dressed in his suit and his tie was hanging loosely around his neck. "What's going on, Gary?" his father asked in a weary voice.

"Why don't *you* tell me?" Gary snapped. "You and Mom are the ones with all the problems these days. Why don't *you* tell *me* what's going on? Huh?"

His father looked surprised. He rubbed his forehead, as if he had a bad headache.

"I was just…upset," Gary said slowly, already regretting his outburst. "I couldn't sleep. Then, when I woke up, I was already late for school. So I decided to take the day off."

"Hey, I can relate," his father yawned. "I don't think I've slept for months. But you just can't take the day off school. What were we supposed to tell your principal? He hauled us into his office and demanded we tell him what was going on. Do you know what that was like?"

"I'm sorry," Gary told his dad. "I didn't think Mr. Bernard would call you and Mom. I just didn't feel like talking to anyone today. Anyway, I'm sorry."

"I guess I'm supposed to punish you now," Gary's father frowned. "But you know what? I don't blame you. I wish I could skip work, too, some days. Especially lately." They both stared at the backyard in silence.

"I guess we better start working on the rink one of these days," Donny said, giving Gary a light tap on the shoulder.

"Dad, can I go to the game tonight?" Gary asked.

"What game?"

"The opening game for the Snow Dogs," Gary answered. Obviously his father didn't have any plans for a father-son outing. He didn't even know it was going on.

"Sure," Donny mumbled on his way into the house. A few minutes later, he peered out the door again. "By the way, what happened to Todd's arm?"

Gary frowned. "A bad sprain. I did it in practice. Checked him too hard."

Donny looked surprised. "What possessed you to do that?"

"I was trying to hit Justin Johnston. He called me MacWuss. Said I was too small for AAA," Gary explained. "I had Justin lined up for the check and then Todd skated in. I hit him instead."

Donny shook his head as he made his way back out onto the step. He looked hard at his son. "That's not what checking is supposed to be about. I didn't raise you to be a bully."

"Well, if you were there to help coach the team, maybe I would have known better," Gary snapped.

"I've got too much on my plate right now," Donny

answered, a look of anger passing across his face. "Your mother's theatrics are all I can handle. I don't need this crap from you, too."

Gary glared back at his father. This wasn't the reaction he had expected. Donny turned back to the door and then paused.

"Gary?"

"Yes?"

"I'm sorry. It's not your fault." Gary was surprised to see tears in his father's eyes as he turned around to face him again. "I don't know what to say. I just can't get anything right these days."

"I'm sorry, too," Gary said softly. "About everything."

His father nodded. "It will get better. With time. But she's not coming back. I know that now."

Gary was startled by his father's honesty. He didn't know what to say.

"I was kidding myself," Donny continued. "I thought she'd be back in a month or two. But when I saw her downtown…"

"Dad, you don't have to tell me all of this."

"But I do. It feels good to talk. We haven't talked enough lately…," he paused. "I guess I thought talking about it would just make it hurt more." He seemed suddenly embarrassed. "Well, I'd better get back to work. Can you and Maggie fend for yourselves tonight?" Gary nodded.

As Gary watched his dad go, he noticed how his father's usually broad shoulders seemed to sag and the patches of grey hair at his temples had grown substantially larger. Gary sighed. How could he even begin to talk to him about Todd's arm, or even about his own feelings about the split? Donny

MacDonald was too wrapped up in his own problems to handle anyone else's. Gary took one last look at the rinkless backyard. He might as well give up.

THE EVENING HADN'T worked out exactly as planned. After his dad left, Gary had gone inside to call Todd. He could go to the opening game after all!

Todd sounded surprised to hear Gary's voice. "I was sure you'd be grounded," he told his friend. "Wasn't your dad mad?"

"Oh, sure," Gary replied, "but he can't get too mad at me right now after what he and my mom have done. So he said I could go to the game. What time should we meet?"

"Uh, there's a problem," Todd mumbled. "I told my dad you couldn't go. He said he would come with me. And, well, he wasn't too happy that I'd asked you in the first place."

Gary was dumbfounded. "Why?"

"Oh, you know. Because of my arm. I mean, I told him it was an accident. And he knows I'll only be out for a couple of weeks, but he's still a little mad at you."

"Have a good time at the game," Gary said curtly. "Besides, I was at the Civic Centre helping the trainer all day. So it's not as if I really need to go to the game. See you around." He quickly slammed down the phone.

For the next couple of hours, Gary had contemplated heading down to the arena and sneaking in the players' entrance. He was sure that Gunner wouldn't mind, but he didn't want to let Todd see him. Suddenly, he felt guilty, again. Nothing was going right!

And so, Gary found himself huddled in the garage, listening to the game on the radio. Maggie was out with her friends and his dad still wasn't home from work. During a lull in the action, Gary thought back on his conversation with his father. He realized his dad hadn't said anything to help him with the Justin problem. As usual, he was too busy feeling sorry for himself. Gary felt the anger welling up inside of him. After all, his mother had hurt him, too.

Why couldn't things just go back to the way they used to be? Gary looked up at the rafters of the garage, where all the boards for the rink were stored away. Just then, the Snow Dogs scored a goal and the crowd at the Civic Centre went nuts. Gary could picture Todd pumping his bandaged arm in the air, cheering for Darby Sanders. He slammed off the radio and went upstairs to bed.

Around four o'clock in the morning, he woke up to the sound of the TV in the family room, still on downstairs. He snuck carefully down the stairs to investigate. His father was asleep in the easy chair. A picture frame had slipped out of his hands onto his lap—their last family picture, taken the Christmas before. Gary turned sadly and went back up to bed. He had hockey practice tomorrow. He needed some sleep.

 **5** DMITRI

WHEN GARY CAME DOWN to breakfast on Saturday morning, his dad was still asleep. Gary asked Maggie to drive him over to the Civic Centre.

"What time's practice?" she asked as she passed her brother the orange juice.

"Four," he mumbled.

Maggie laughed. "It's only ten o'clock. Why are you going over so early?"

"I thought I'd just hang around there for the day. Maybe the Snow Dogs are around," he said, hoping his sister wouldn't tease him.

"They're on the road this weekend," Maggie told him in that know-it-all voice that drove Gary nuts.

"They left this morning for New Brunswick. They've got games tonight and Sunday night against the Saint John Flames."

Gary stared at his sister. "Since when do you care so much about the Snow Dogs? You hardly know your own team's schedule, never mind the AHL's."

Maggie blushed. "Well, everyone's talking about them. I went to the game last night with my friends. It was pretty cool. I was surprised you weren't there."

Gary felt a surge of anger. This was just adding insult to injury, he thought.

"I saw Todd," Maggie continued, not noticing her brother's response. "What happened to his arm?"

"It's just a sprain," Gary snapped. "I wish everybody would stop making such a big deal out of it." He decided not to mention how Todd got his injury. The last thing he needed was another lecture.

Maggie stared at her brother for a minute, then changed the subject. "I'm going to stay over at Mom's tonight. Why don't you come over after practice."

"I don't really feel like spending too much time with her right now, thanks." Gary spat out the words in the coldest voice he could manage.

"Oh, you'd rather spend time with our father, Mr. Happiness," Maggie shot back.

"He's not the one who decided that we weren't worth living with," Gary argued.

"Whoa...it's not like we have to pick sides here," Maggie cautioned. "They're both having a hard time."

"Sure," Gary mumbled. He paused for a moment, then decided to let his sister in on the conversation he'd had yesterday with their father.

"He actually talked about it," Gary said tentatively.

Maggie raised her eyebrows. "He did? When?"

"Yesterday, after I skipped...after he and Mom met with Mr. Bernard at Stonepark."

"Oh yeah, I heard about that," his sister giggled.

"So, he's reaming me out for acting like a bully, and all of a sudden he tells me he thought Mom wasn't going to come back. And he said he didn't want to talk about it because it hurt too much."

Gary looked at his sister for some reaction.

"That's good, I guess," Maggie said cautiously. She looked at the stairs to make sure their dad wasn't listening in. "I do feel sorry for him. But at the same time, I wish he'd just try to move on...so we can all move on."

Gary shrugged. "I don't think it was easy for him to tell me that much. Maybe he is getting better."

After breakfast, Gary hauled his equipment into the minivan and they set off for the arena.

"So what about coming to Mom's place?" Maggie asked again as they got closer to their destination.

Gary shook his head. "No way."

He jumped out of the minivan as soon as they reached the Civic Centre. "Thanks for the ride," he muttered, eyes down. He slammed the door shut.

Maggie looked through the passenger window at her brother, worried crinkles creasing her forehead. Gary gave her a grateful look and waved as she drove away. Although she got on his nerves once in a while, he knew she was about the coolest sister he could hope to have, considering she was a girl. She liked sports and gave him his space, and since their parents split up, Maggie had become his main source of support—and he hers. They could only really talk to each other about what was going on. Things were still too fresh to share with anyone else.

The Civic Centre was a mess. Programs and garbage were strewn around the parking lot and the entranceway, and Gary stopped to pick up a program to replace the one he'd dropped yesterday morning. He made sure no one was watching, and then stuffed it in his hockey bag. He made his way into the Civic Centre and headed toward his team's dressing room to drop off his equipment. The hallways were empty. Obviously, everyone had had a late night. Gary turned a corner and almost bumped into a tall, dark-haired guy in a faded jean jacket. The young man was staring intently at a map of Charlottetown. He had a duffel bag at his feet and Gary noticed a tag marked with strange writing.

The young man looked up, his face wrinkled in concentration. He broke into a grin when he saw Gary. "I am...lost," he said in a thick accent. "Can you help me?"

Gary nodded, racking his brain to figure out who this guy was. Obviously a hockey player from somewhere in Eastern Europe, but who? Suddenly, it clicked. The *Guardian* had reported that Dmitri Rushkov was joining the club. Rushkov was one of the rising stars in the Snow Dogs organization. He had been one of the NHL team's last cuts, despite being just eighteen with no previous professional experience.

"You're Dmitri Rushkov," Gary said, his voice rising with excitement. The Russian looked surprised.

"You know me?"

"Sure," Gary replied. "You played for the Russian junior team that won gold at the world championships. You were drafted in the top ten."

Rushkov looked embarrassed. He waved the map of Charlottetown at Gary. "I need to find apartment. This—this is where?" He pointed on the map to Euston Street.

"I know where that is," Gary said enthusiastically. "It's close to where I live. I could take you."

Dmitri pointed to the emblem on Gary's jacket. "You are hockey player too?" he asked, smiling.

"Yes. I mean, not for the Snow Dogs. I mean, I play for the Abbies," Gary was flustered. What was a big star like Dmitri Rushkov doing talking to him?

"And what is your name?" Dmitri continued. Gary noticed that the player's English got better as he relaxed.

"I'm Gary. Gary MacDonald." Dmitri put out his arm and the two shook hands.

"Pleased to meet you. I am Dmitri Rushkov," Dmitri said formally. Then he picked up his duffel bag. "You help me find apartment now?"

Just then, a blonde woman in a suit came racing around the corner, waving a cellphone. "Dmitri, Dmitri," she shouted. She put the cellphone to her ear. "I've found him. I'll call you back when he's on his way." She slammed the phone shut.

"I'm Cheryl Porter, media relations." Dmitri shook hands with her, looking slightly confused. "There has been a terrible mistake," she continued. "You were supposed to meet the team in Saint John! I had no idea you were coming or I would have been at the airport. I'm terribly sorry."

Dmitri looked even more baffled. He turned to Gary for help. Cheryl Porter gave Gary a dismissive glance and turned back to the hockey player. She took him by the arm. "We've got to hurry. We can get you on a flight to New Brunswick in twenty minutes. They need you there for tonight's game."

The woman steered Dmitri toward the door. He stopped and looked back at Gary. "Thank you for your help, Gary MacDonald." The Russian grinned and gave a playful shrug as the media relations woman pushed him out the door. Gary was left standing by himself.

Wow, he thought, I just shook hands with Dmitri Rushkov! Too bad he hadn't had a chance to help the Russian star find his apartment. Still, just talking to the young player had been a thrill.

GARY WAS SITTING in his gear, waiting, when the first of his teammates arrived for practice. He was still in a good mood. After his encounter with the Russian hockey star, nothing was going to ruin his day. Justin Johnston swaggered over and playfully punched Gary in the arm.

"Hey, MacWuss, who ya gonna take out this practice? I'm sure Manning will enjoy watching our game on Tuesday from the stands. Thanks to you, of course." Gary got up and headed toward the door.

"Good thing you got him though, MacWuss," Johnston taunted. "If he was here, you wouldn't be. You were on the way to AA until Manning got hurt. Oh well, I'm sure you'll be heading there soon enough."

"Yeah, MacWuss." It was Mike Bartlett's turn to chime in. "At least Manning *looks* like he's in junior high, you little punk. Hope you start growing soon, short stuff. We're getting tired of having a pipsqueak like you take up a spot on our team."

The boys burst into laughter and walked away, high-fiving each other as they went.

Gary's ears were burning as he headed for the ice. He stood there, shaking with anger, until the Zamboni finished its work. He looked over at the stands and saw Todd sitting with his dad. Gary turned away. He hoped Mr. Manning couldn't see him.

The assistant coaches put the boys through their paces while Coach Mulligan watched from the stands. With only fifteen minutes left in practice, he joined them on the ice.

"You're all going to have to do better than this if we want to win," Mulligan roared. "Many of you are first-year players, and you're in for a rough ride. We've already lost one player to injury. I want the rest of you to keep your heads up. And *no stupid checks*. Yes, the Abbies are a tough team. But we play clean. Am I understood?"

The Coach paused. Justin nodded in Gary's direction and raised his eyebrows. Some of the other players snickered.

"Our first game is Tuesday. I want you boys to sleep and eat hockey between now and then. Let's get this season off to a good start. That's it."

The Coach skated off and Gary breathed a sigh of relief. He was still on the team. Now all he had to worry about was the competition. He had until Tuesday to figure out how he was going to survive.

HE SHOOTS, HE SEES STARS 6

AT SUPPER THAT NIGHT, Gary told his father and Maggie about meeting Dmitri Rushkov. Even his dad seemed impressed.

"That kid's going places. He's headed to the NHL for sure," Donny commented, passing the pizza box to his son.

The MacDonalds were having pizza—again. Neither Gary nor his dad had mentioned their fight. Both were acting as if it never happened and Gary was just fine with that. No one commented on the fact that Maggie had spent the weekend with her mother either. If this is denial, Gary thought, we're all getting really good at it.

"We should have Dmitri over for supper some time!" Donny suggested.

"Oh yeah, like an NHL star wants to have pizza with us?" Maggie snickered.

"No, wait," Donny replied, shooting Maggie a look of mock anger. "The Snow Dogs are having an Adopt-a-Player campaign and my firm is involved. If we adopted Dmitri, we could have him over for supper. And since when did you start complaining about having pizza?"

"When we started having it every single night," his daughter teased.

"Dad, that would be so cool," Gary piped in. "He seems like a really nice guy. And he doesn't know very much English. We could help him."

"This guy makes millions of dollars," Maggie interjected. "Why would he want to have supper with a bunch of no-names like us?"

"He doesn't make millions yet," her father corrected. "And Gary's right. Just put yourself in his shoes. He's only eighteen. He's just arrived in a strange country where he doesn't know the language. I'm sure he could use a friendly face or two."

Gary nodded enthusiastically, but secretly wondered if his father would follow through on his promise. Donny hadn't exactly been himself lately, and Gary didn't want to get his hopes up, just to be disappointed again.

He didn't have to wait long to find out. At Sunday night's dinner, Donny announced that his law firm had selected Dmitri Rushkov as their player. "The Snow Dogs said they weren't sure how long he'd be down in the minors, but they were happy to set it up at least for now. After all, the firm *did* buy ten season tickets," he said with a wink.

"So, what next?" Maggie asked, perking up at the news. She had looked up Dmitri in the team program and decided that he was kind of cute. Suddenly, she was much more interested in the plan.

"We talk to the media relations person—a Cheryl Porter," her father explained. "Some companies will have the players sign autographs and attend special events. But in our case, we'll just invite him over for supper and see how it goes."

"How about later this week? They're back in town," Gary suggested. "And you know what? He lives over on Euston Street, so it's really close."

"What about the day after tomorrow?" Maggie said eagerly.

Gary shook his head. "I've got my first game Tuesday night. At Sherwood."

Gary felt his stomach lurch at the thought. The Sherwood Kings had finished runners-up in the province last season, second only to the Abbies. Most of their players were returning and the team was expected to give the Abbies a serious run for the championship. The entire league knew that the Abbies had a young lineup this season, and Coach Mulligan said everyone was gunning for them. As the game grew closer, Gary grew more and more nervous about his bantam debut.

"Okay, how about Friday night then?" Gary's dad asked. "Do you have a game or practice?"

Gary shook his head. He couldn't believe that his dad didn't even know his schedule. It was posted on the fridge right next to Maggie's—there for the entire family to see. When his dad used to coach, he knew exactly when Gary's games were. Now he just wasn't interested.

FINALLY, TUESDAY EVENING arrived. Gary's hands were sweating as he pulled on his jersey and laced up his skates. Coach Mulligan gave one final pep talk.

"Most of you boys have grown up as Abbies. And so you know about this club's winning tradition. But it's even more important than ever now. You're playing bantam AAA. This is a big year for those of you who want to go on in hockey. Make it your best one."

With that, he guided the team out onto the ice at the Sherwood Sportsplex. As he skated around in warm-up, Gary scanned the stands. His heart sank as he spotted Todd and Mr. Manning in the crowd. Todd gave Gary an encouraging smile but Gary looked away. Just as the warm-up was ending, he saw his dad and Maggie arrive. He gave them a quick wave.

Gary didn't play much in the first period, which gave him more time to sit on the bench and get nervous. The Abbies fell behind by a couple of goals. Between periods, Coach Mulligan pulled Gary aside. "I'm going to move you up to the second line, MacDonald," he rasped, chomping on his cigar. "Are you ready?" Gary nodded.

The Kings kept the Abbies in their own end for most of the second period, but Gary finally wriggled past the defence and got a shot on goal. "Good shift," Coach Mulligan told him as he returned to the bench. "Don't be afraid to go high."

The next time he stepped on the ice, Gary felt more confident. Maybe the Kings weren't so good after all. He got the puck at centre ice and skated in. The big defender tried to throw a check and missed. Gary zipped past and in on the net. He put the puck high. The Abbies' bench went wild. It was now 3–1 for Sherwood.

During the break between periods, Gary noticed Justin glowering in his direction. He smiled to himself, but his smile quickly faded as the team headed back onto the ice for the third period. Justin's dad was standing at ice level, just behind the net. Bud Johnston roared at his son as Justin skated to the Abbies' bench.

"Get yer ass in gear, boy," Johnston shouted. "Those lousy refs aren't going to call a thing, so get in there and do your stuff."

In the third period, Coach Mulligan put Gary on the power play a couple of times and he had a few more shots on net. With five minutes left to play, he managed to get a break-away with Justin trailing. He waited until the last possible minute to pass to his teammate, pulling the goalie with him. Justin had an open net to shoot at and easily scored.

"Nice pass," Justin said reluctantly as they headed to the bench. Gary saw the older player look over to the glass. Bud Johnston was exchanging high-fives with some of the other fathers.

"Good unselfish play, MacDonald," the Coach praised him. "Okay boys, we're down by just one now. Let's put it to them."

On his next shift, Gary noticed that the Sherwood players were shadowing him much more than usual. He received a pass and started toward the Kings' end. The hit took him by surprise. His legs went out from under him and he went fly-ing in the air. The whistle blew and the ref skated over to where Gary was lying on the ice, trying to catch his breath.

"You okay?" the ref asked. Gary nodded his head as he tentatively got to his feet. There was a smattering of applause as Gary headed for the bench. As he looked up at the crowd, he was surprised to see his mother sitting in the stands. She looked worried. He gave her a reassuring smile and she smiled back.

"Gary, what day is it?" Gordie, the trainer, leaned over Gary, waving his hands in front of Gary's eyes.

"Tuesday," Gary replied.

"Where are we?" Gordie asked.

"Sherwood Sportsplex," Gary answered, trying to look past Gordie at the action on the ice. "Sit still, will you? I just have to check for a possible concussion," the trainer said. "You smacked your head pretty hard."

"MacDonald, you're sitting for the rest of the game," the Coach told him. Gary tried to protest but Mulligan walked away. When he looked up at the stands again, his mother had left. He saw his father and sister over at the other side of the arena. He wondered if they had noticed Martha MacDonald.

After the game, Gary's head was throbbing. When he came out of the dressing room, his dad and Maggie were waiting.

"Hey, great game," Maggie said.

"Great debut, Gary," his dad added, taking his hockey bag. "How's the head? That was quite a hit."

Coach Mulligan came out of the dressing room. "MacDonald, I want you to see a doctor before next practice."

"What for?" Gary asked, perplexed. "I've got a headache, that's all."

"That's one of the symptoms of a concussion. You get it checked out, you hear?"

Mulligan turned to Gary's father. "He had quite a game until the hit. He's got the magic touch around the net. I was worried that he was too small—and I could still be proved right—but he's got the makings of a goal scorer, alright, and that's what this team needs this year."

"Remember what I said," he concluded, waving his cigar at Gary. "No doctor, no practice." Coach Mulligan disappeared back into the dressing room.

ON WEDNESDAY, Gary went to see Dr. Champion after school. She'd been his family doctor since he was born. "Everything okay at school?" she asked, as she looked in his eyes and ears.

"Sure," Gary mumbled.

"You must be excited about the Snow Dogs." Dr. Champion took his pulse as she talked.

"Yeah, they're cool," Gary replied. He anxiously awaited the doctor's verdict.

"Tell me more about your headache," the doctor said, wrapping up the blood pressure cuff.

"It was no big deal. I just took some Tylenol." Gary replied. "This morning it was gone."

He wasn't being entirely honest. This afternoon at school his eyes had throbbed and he'd felt dizzy for a minute or two. But that had passed, so he had decided not to mention it.

"Alright." Dr. Champion made some notes in the folder holding his medical records. "You're okay to go back to practice. But if the headaches come back, or you feel dizzy, or anything like that, you come back to see me. And no more whacks to the head!"

Gary rushed over to the Civic Centre. He was a few minutes late for practice. He threw on his gear and headed out to centre ice. Coach Mulligan was already talking to the team. He turned to Gary and filled him in. "I think we need to get you an enforcer, so to speak. I've asked Johnston to keep an eye out for anyone who's trying to get to you."

Gary looked surprised. "Are you okay to play?" the Coach continued. Gary nodded. "Alright then, you're on the first line with MacKenzie and Currie. You guys put on the red jerseys and we'll get started. Second line in green, third in blue. Let's go."

Gary snuck a look over in Justin's direction. The older boy looked grim. "I'm just doing this because I have to, MacWuss. If you weren't such a wuss…"

The Coach blew his whistle and Gary skated over to join his new linemates. Only when practice was over did he have a chance to digest the news. He was on the first line for the Abbies! Wait until his dad heard about this.

As he was leaving the arena, Russ, the assistant coach, pulled Gary aside. He handed Gary a piece of paper. "We've put together a personalized weights program for you," he explained. "We want you to bulk up as much as you can… until you grow," he added kindly. "We can't have those guys hitting you around. A couple of concussions and you'll be out of commission for the season. Or worse." Russ gave Gary a reassuring smile. "You're a natural, kid. If you grow, you could do well."

Gary walked out of the Civic Centre, his emotions churning. He had been excited about moving up to the first line, but now he was more frustrated than anything else. Everyone kept telling him how good he was, but they also kept harping on his size. What if he never grew? He remembered Coach Mulligan's advice about power versus skill. He decided to make a list of small players in the NHL who had made it despite their size. Like Wayne Gretzky, he thought proudly. Gary rubbed his head. He could feel a hint of a headache coming on again. He would get to the weights after supper. Maybe he'd feel better by then.

THE REST OF THE WEEK seemed to drag by. Donny had called Cheryl Porter and extended their invitation to Dmitri. He was supposed to come over on Friday night. It was a day off for the players before a big weekend series against the St. John's Maple Leafs. The MacDonalds were told to expect Dmitri around six.

Gary went to the gym after school and it was almost six o'clock by the time he arrived home. His father was just getting out of the minivan and Maggie was nowhere to be seen. Gary gasped as he walked into the house and looked around the kitchen. There were dishes everywhere and the entire place was filthy. There were dirty clothes everywhere, including his smelly hockey jerseys piled along the railing going upstairs. Suddenly, the doorbell rang.

Dmitri was wearing a shirt and tie under his jean jacket and he was carrying flowers. He smiled broadly as he recognized Gary.

"Gary MacDonald, from the arena," Dmitri grinned. "I did not know it was your family. These are for your mother."

Gary didn't know what to say. He stared blankly at the flowers as Maggie came down the stairs. She was wearing a short jean skirt, a pair of wedge sandals and makeup. Gary held back giggles as Maggie shyly took the flowers from Dmitri. She elbowed Gary.

"This is my sister, Maggie," Gary explained. The two shook hands. "Our mother is, uh..."

"She doesn't live here anymore," Maggie blurted out. She gave her father a nervous look. Donny MacDonald stepped forward and introduced himself.

"Please excuse the mess, Dmitri," Donny said jovially. "We're on our own, the three of us, so the house doesn't get cleaned as often as it should."

Gary and Maggie quickly cleaned off the dining room table and set out some plates. Donny carried in the pizzas and pointed Dmitri to a chair.

"As you can see, we also eat well here," Donny laughed. Gary was embarrassed until he saw Dmitri's eyes light up.

"I love pizza. I cannot eat enough pizza," he explained. He watched as Donny MacDonald took off his jacket and loosened his tie. Dmitri quickly did the same.

AS THE PIZZA DISAPPEARED, the MacDonalds and their guest warmed up. Dmitri told them about growing up and playing hockey in Moscow.

"My country does not have very much money for sports," he explained. "There is no money to heat arenas and our equipment is very old."

"But you keep winning!" Gary exclaimed, mesmerized by the Russian player's every word. He was growing used to Dmitri's accent and was often able to help the young Russian find the word he was looking for.

"Yes, we win, but that is because we do nothing but play hockey," Dmitri replied. "I played for the Red Army team and they paid me. It was not lots of money, but enough for me and my mother and brother to live and eat."

"What about school?" Maggie asked.

Dmitri shook his head. "School was not so important. I was a hockey player. My team would make good money when I went to NHL."

Gary looked over at his father, confused. Donny MacDonald explained. "When Dmitri was drafted, the Red Army team and Russia received compensation from the NHL. That's where these teams get most of their money these days, by producing players who leave Russia to play in the NHL."

"So why don't you have good equipment and big arenas?" Gary persisted.

"My government is still very, how do you say—corrupt," Dmitri said sadly. "My mother worked for many years in a factory. When the factory closed, she received no money. The government doesn't care. So I go to play hockey to support my mother and Pavel."

Dmitri smiled at the mention of his brother. He pointed to Gary. "You remember me of Pavel," he said.

"I remind you of your brother?"

"You remind me, yes," Dmitri grinned. "He is one year more young from me. He plays hockey for Red Army. He was drafted also. But he is not wanting to come to Canada."

"Why not?" Maggie asked Dmitri, blushing slightly when he turned to look at her. "He want to stay and take care of my mother," Dmitri shrugged. "He says he likes Russia."

Gary noticed that Dmitri never mentioned his father. He wondered what had happened to him. Gary frowned when he realized that he never mentioned his mother, either. Maybe Dmitri's parents were divorced, too. He shuddered slightly at the word. He still hoped that his parents would be able to work out their problems, but he was beginning to wonder if that was even possible. His mom had practically disappeared from his father's life.

Maggie got up from the table to clear the plates. Gary grabbed Dmitri's plate just as Maggie tried to reach it, almost knocking the leftover pizza onto the Russian's lap. Maggie elbowed her brother, her face turning red.

"Hey, two minutes for elbowing," Gary snickered. "She's a great hockey player. Always in the penalty box."

"You play hockey, too?" Dmitri asked, looking surprised. He snuck a look at Maggie teetering on her sandals and raised his eyebrows.

"I love hockey," Maggie said and then rushed to the kitchen to regain her composure. Donny and Gary exchanged amused looks.

"Well, we better let you get home," Donny said. "The New Mexico Snow Dogs are playing tonight on CBC. I bet you'd like to catch the game."

Dmitri looked confused. "The Snow Dogs are playing where?"

"On TV," Gary explained, "You know, on *Hockey Night in Canada*."

Dmitri still looked puzzled. "I do not know this *Hockey Night*. I have no television."

"No TV!" Gary exclaimed. "I was sure you'd have a big screen with stereo speakers."

Dmitri looked to Donny for an explanation. Gary's father shook his head, laughing. "It's a North American custom. The bigger your TV, the better," he chuckled.

"Why don't you watch the game here," Gary suggested.

Dmitri looked pleased. "I would like that very much. My apartment, she is very small. And very quiet, so I am very homesick when I am there."

Dmitri stayed and watched the game. It was after eleven o'clock by the time he left. The MacDonalds stood at the door, and everyone, including Maggie, formally shook hands with Dmitri as he prepared to head home.

"You come see me play tomorrow," he said to all of them. "I ask Cheryl to give you tickets."

"I've got plans, but I'm sure Gary and Maggie would love to go," Donny replied. "And maybe you can come and watch them play sometime."

"Or maybe even come to one of my practices!" Gary exclaimed enthusiastically.

His sister elbowed him. "I'm sure Dmitri is busy..." she hissed. The Russian player waved his hands to interject.

"No, I am not so busy. I would like very much to come to your practice and game someday. We will talk again soon."

THE NEXT DAY, Cheryl Porter called to say that Dmitri had left four tickets at the box office. "Dmitri seemed really happy to have met all of you," she told Gary, in a much warmer voice than the one she'd used during their first encounter. "I'm sure he'll be heading to New Mexico soon, but having someone he knows here in Charlottetown will really make the transition to life in North America much easier."

After he hung up, Gary wondered about what the public relations woman had said. He tried to imagine what it was like for Dmitri, coming to a new country where he didn't know anyone or speak the language. He suspected that life in Albuquerque, New Mexico, was going to be even more complicated. A big American city would be a challenge compared to sleepy old Charlottetown. Still, Dmitri would be playing in the NHL—a dream that Gary and all the boys he knew secretly shared. Suddenly, the phone rang again. Gary picked it up, expecting it to be Cheryl Porter calling back for some reason. Instead he heard his mother offer a tentative, "Hello."

"How's the head?" she asked, trying her best to sound cheerful.

"Okay," Gary mumbled.

"Maggie tells me that you have a new friend."

"Mmmm," Gary replied uncooperatively. He twiddled the cord of the phone line, feeling uncomfortable.

"Do you have plans for tonight?" his mother asked.

"Yep," he answered. "Todd and me are going to the game."

"Todd and I..." his mother started to correct him and then stopped. "I just wanted to make sure your head was okay. You had a good game the other night," she added.

Gary felt a wave of pleasure despite his determination to be cool. He quickly said goodbye and hung up the phone.

Maggie and one of her friends took one set of tickets, and Gary invited Todd to come with him. Gary had always been a Leafs fan growing up, but now he was cheering against his old favourites. He watched with excitement as the Snow Dogs came out for their warm-up.

"And number 8, Dmitri Rushkov," the announcer boomed

and the crowd cheered. Dmitri was already a fan favourite. He was the team's leading scorer even though he had missed the first couple of games of the season. Everyone knew that Rushkov was headed to the NHL someday soon and they were anxious to watch a future star play.

Darby Sanders was another of the crowd's favourites. The team captain led the Snow Dogs in penalty minutes and the fans loved to cheer him on when he got into a shoving match with the tough guys from the other teams. Rob Duffy, the tall blonde that Gary had met the first day of practice, was one of the most controversial players. He had been benched for a couple of games for violating the team's curfew, and there were rumours that he was out late every night at Myron's, one of the city's main drinking spots. Todd's dad said that Duffy had even been caught driving drunk, but the cop decided not to give him a ticket because he recognized him as a Snow Dogs player.

"Look at all the empty seats," Todd said during one of the breaks in the first period.

"I don't get it," Gary said, munching on a handful of popcorn. He and Todd had great seats, just behind the penalty box across from the team benches. Gary tried to catch Dmitri's eye but the young Russian was deep in concentration, even on the bench.

"I mean, this is a big deal—having a farm club here," Todd continued. "Why aren't people coming out to the games?"

"I thought they'd be sold out all the time," Gary agreed. "I guess the tickets are kind of expensive." He looked at his ticket stub. His seat would have cost fifteen dollars. That was thirty bucks for a couple, even more for a family. Still, one of their friends from school had gone to a game at the new arena where the Maple Leafs played in Toronto. He said those tickets had been almost ninety dollars apiece.

"What's Dmitri like? Is he full of himself like Duffy?" Todd asked. His father's company had invited Duffy to a fundraising event as part of its sponsorship of the Snow Dogs. Duffy had shown up late and Mr. Manning hinted that he might have been drinking before he arrived. The company had not been impressed, though they had worked hard to keep any negative publicity away from the media.

Gary shook his head vehemently. "He's really cool! He talks with this great accent and every once in a while he gets his words all confused. He's not stuck-up at all. You know what? He doesn't even have a TV. He stayed at our house and watched *Hockey Night in Canada*."

Todd was as amazed as Gary had been. "Why doesn't he have a TV?"

Gary shrugged. "He sends all his money back to Russia to help his mom and brother. His brother Pavel is a year younger and was drafted too."

Todd looked impressed. "So Dmitri doesn't have one of those fancy sport-utility vehicles like the rest of the guys?"

"Nope, and no gold chains or leather jackets," Gary snickered. He thought back to the first day of practice and the players speeding out of the parking lot.

"I guess you can't blame them," Todd remarked as the period ended. The boys got out of their seats and looked around the arena. "This isn't exactly the big leagues. Who would want to be in dumb old Charlottetown when you could be in New Mexico and in the NHL?"

"Yeah, but they should save their money," Gary insisted. "What happens if they don't make it to the NHL, or end up playing for just a couple of games?" He and Todd watched as Socky Mulligan drove out on the Zamboni and started to clean the ice. His NHL dream didn't last very long. Gary wondered what Socky thought of the young upstarts who strutted around the arena acting as if they had the world at their feet just because they were playing in the American Hockey League.

"Hey, Gary!" a voice shouted.

Gary turned and saw Gunner carrying a bag-load of sticks into the dressing room. "Come by some time, kid," Gunner yelled, his voice kind despite his usual fierce expression. "Dmitri asked me to put aside a couple of sticks for you. But keep it quiet." The trainer gave the boys a big wink and disappeared into the dressing room.

"Cool!" Todd exclaimed. As the boys continued past the dressing room, they noticed a group of girls hovering around. He was surprised to see Maggie and some of her friends there. He noticed his sister looked uncomfortable. The rest of the girls were fixing their hair or makeup, looking anxiously over to the dressing room door. Maggie was standing at the back of the group, though her friend was trying to nudge her closer.

"Puck bunny alert!" Todd whispered. Gary frowned. He didn't like to see his sister hanging around with the girls who chased after the hockey players. Why was Maggie wasting her time with this bunch? Almost all of the girls there were still in high school. Gary couldn't imagine what they thought a hockey player would see in them.

The Snow Dogs won by a score of 3–2. Dmitri had two goals and was named the game's first star. When he skated out to wave to the crowd, he looked over at Gary and Todd and waved. Gary waved back wildly, hoping that everyone in the stands noticed.

When Gary got back from the arena, the house was empty. He was surprised that his dad wasn't there. Donny had been sticking close to home since his wife had moved out. Gary wondered sleepily where his dad was so late at night. Later on, he fell asleep with a smile on his face, replaying the Snow Dogs' game winner over and over in his mind—but in his dream, he scored the winning goal.

GETTING TOUGH 8

WHEN GARY GOT downstairs the next morning, Maggie was storming around the kitchen, slamming cupboard doors.

"What's your problem?" Gary asked lightly.

His sister just glared at him. "None of your business," she snapped.

"How was the game?" their father asked, appearing in the doorway. He was wearing a jacket and jeans and looked like he was going out. Gary noticed that his dad was smiling.

"Great! We won 3–2 and Dmitri had two goals," Gary replied. Maggie was silent, slumped into a kitchen chair. Her father looked over at her with raised eyebrows.

"Oh yes, the great Dmitri," she said scornfully.

"What's that supposed to mean?" Gary asked.

"Oh, Mr. 'I'm So Lonely' certainly wasn't lonely last night," Maggie snarled. "He invited a whole crowd of girls over to his apartment last night. He and that Rob Duffy. When they left Myron's, Dmitri had two drunk girls hanging on him. I'm sure he isn't too lonely now."

Donny looked over at his daughter, who lowered her eyes. Gary wondered if his sister realized she had just confessed to being at a bar. He prepared for his father's lecture, but instead, Donny went over and gave his daughter a quick hug. "I'm sorry, honey," he said softly. "I guess we forget some-times that these guys live in a different world. One where they are stars and there are lots of people who just want a piece of a star. I wouldn't be too disappointed that you're not like those girls."

Maggie shrugged. Gary couldn't believe it! His sister was-n't even going to get in trouble! "I'm sure it was all Duffy's idea," Gary told his sister, defending his new friend. "Dmitri was probably just too nice to say no."

"Yeah, whatever," Maggie snarled. "Those hockey players treat all girls like dirt. They think they're so great, just because they're going to play in the NHL."

"Maggie, that's not fair," her father intervened. "Dmitri has been very nice to us. Maybe you misunderstood..."

"Dad, I heard Duffy telling Dmitri that those girls would do whatever he wanted. Dmitri just smiled," Maggie insisted.

Gary was starting to squirm. He didn't want to believe Maggie's story. It just didn't sound like Dmitri.

"Well, they're out of town now, so we'll have to wait to ask Dmitri what was really going on," Gary said.

"You've got to be kidding," Maggie muttered. "I'm sure Mr. High and Mighty won't have time for some stupid kid when he gets back. Leave him alone, Gary. He's bad news."

Donny looked at his watch and started toward the door. "Can you two take care of things here for the day? I'm going out for a drive along the North Shore. There's money on the counter for supper."

"Who're you going with?" Maggie asked, munching a mouthful of peanut butter and toast.

"A friend," Donny replied cryptically. "I'm late. Got to go. Don't fight. Oh, and Gary, have a great practice. We'll have to start working on the rink soon, won't we?"

Their father pulled the door shut behind him as Gary and Maggie exchanged puzzled looks.

"Do you think he and Mom are going for a drive?" Gary asked hopefully.

Maggie shook her head. "Nope. But I answered the phone the other day and it was someone asking for Dad. A woman."

Gary stared at his sister in surprise. "Who was it?"

"Somebody from work. Her name's Lisa. She's left a message on the machine a couple of times, too" Maggie explained.

Gary looked relieved. "So they're just working. It's not like a date or anything."

"Oh no, I think it's a date. She sounded very friendly and teased him about not calling her back. She said something about getting him to show her around the Island. It sounds like she just moved here."

Gary tossed his toast back on his plate. "I don't believe it. How could Dad be so stupid?"

"What do you mean 'stupid'? Is he supposed to be in mourning for the rest of his life?"

"Mom and Dad have just split up. And he was so upset that Mom was dating and now he's going out on a date, too!"

"Gary, give it a rest, okay? If it means he's not so cranky, he can date the Queen of England for all I care."

Maggie got up from the table, leaving her brother to fume over his breakfast.

He was still sitting there, ten minutes later, when she came back into the kitchen, carrying her knapsack. "Are you ready to go? I need to study—so if you want a ride to practice, it's now or never."

Both were silent as they headed to the minivan, and the drive was no better. Maggie finally broke the silence as the Civic Centre came into view. "I'm sorry about what I said. And I know you're right about Dmitri. I was just mad because Angela dragged me to that stupid bar. And I felt like an idiot standing there with all those girls."

"I really don't think he's like that," Gary insisted. "And don't worry. You couldn't be a puck bunny if you tried."

They both laughed.

"Hey, let's rake the yard later," Maggie suggested as they pulled into the parking lot. "We've still got lots of time to get the boards ready. The rink will get done. Don't worry."

Gary gave his sister a grin as he jumped out of the minivan and grabbed his hockey gear. He slid the door shut and almost crashed into Todd's father, who was helping his son unload his hockey gear from the back of their truck.

"Hey, you're back," Gary said, his face brightening up. He avoided looking at Mr. Manning. Todd never mentioned the accident, but Gary knew that some hard feelings remained with Todd's dad. He was miffed that Gary had turned into one of the team's stars while his son sat on the sidelines. Gary was just happy to have his friend back.

Gary and Todd found two spots, side by side, in the locker room. Gary smiled as he began to unload his gear. What a relief to have his best friend next to him again! He had never felt totally comfortable with the older boys, and Todd would be a good ally against the constant teasing from Justin and the others. As they pulled on their pads and taped up, Gary glanced over at the other side of the room where Justin was putting on his equipment. He was wearing a ripped tank top under his shoulder pads and Gary couldn't help but notice his muscles. He quickly pulled on his own jersey, hoping Justin hadn't seen his look. Too late.

"What's the matter, MacWuss? Never seen muscles before?" The other boys snickered. Mike stood up on the bench and flexed his muscles. "See, MacWuss? This is what a real hockey player looks like." He struck another pose and his friends, including Justin, hooted with laughter.

Gary's lack of muscles was a sore point these days. He had religiously followed the training regimen that the team had set out. He lifted weights at home and at the YMCA. He did sit-ups and push-ups until his arms ached. He had even tried eating raw eggs after Todd saw someone in a movie doing it. But nothing worked. Gary was still the smallest player on the team.

"Hey, I can help you with those pathetic arms and legs," Justin said slyly. "Come here."

Justin dug a plastic bag out of his hockey gear. It was filled with pills of every colour and description. He grabbed a handful, put them into another plastic bag and gave them to Gary.

"Here's what you need, MacWuss," Justin told him, keeping an eye on the door. "One of these a day and maybe, if you're lucky, you'll be able to stand up for yourself someday. Then I'll be able to play hockey instead of babysitting you."

Before Gary could ask Justin what the pills were, Russ stuck his head in the door. "Five minutes, boys, let's move it."

Gary shoved the pills into his bag and mumbled his thanks to Justin.

AFTER PRACTICE, Gary and Todd hung around the hallway, waiting for Mrs. Manning to come pick them up.

"You're not going to actually take those pills, are you?" Todd asked nervously.

"Why not? They can't hurt," Gary said, playfully flexing his arm muscle.

"What if they're dangerous or something?" Todd insisted. There was something in Todd's voice that made Gary feel defensive. He was usually so laid-back. What was up with all the questions? Maybe Todd was worried that Gary actually would grow some muscles and finally be able to compete with him in the strength department.

"Johnston's a jerk, but he wouldn't give me anything dangerous. I'm sure they're just some kind of steroid. Lots of people take them."

"But aren't they illegal?" Todd asked. "How did Johnston get them?"

"Shhhh," Gary interrupted his friend. "Somebody's coming."

The two boys slipped into one of the entranceways and listened as a faraway voice got closer and closer. It was Clark Dinsmore, and he sure was yelling at someone.

"I've had it with all the excuses," the former star shouted. "Yes, this is a small market and yes, the tickets are expensive for the average family. But if we don't sell more tickets soon, we're not going to make it through the season. The owners are getting itchy. It's my head on the line. So either you do something fast, or it's your head first."

"I'm doing my best, Mr. Dinsmore." Gary recognized the voice—Cheryl Porter.

"If you want to go anywhere in this organization, I would suggest that you make this work. Otherwise, you'll never get a chance to work in a real market," Dinsmore threatened.

"I don't know what else I can do," Cheryl Porter sounded more than a little upset. "Oh, and there's the problem with Duffy to contend with as well. What am I supposed to do about that?"

"The little ass," Dinsmore fumed, banging his hand against the wall. Both boys jumped, desperately hoping that they weren't about to be caught eavesdropping. "Make it go away. I don't want to know how you do it, just do it," Dinsmore directed his assistant. "We've got a meeting. Let's go."

The boys waited until the sound of the footsteps faded and quickly made their way out of the Civic Centre.

"Did you hear that?" Todd whispered as soon as they were out of the building. "What did they mean about Duffy?"

"I don't know," Gary said, shaking his head. "But Maggie said Duffy and Dmitri had some wild party last night with lots of girls."

"Dmitri?" Todd asked, surprised.

"I don't think it's true," Gary insisted. "I'm sure he was just too nice to tell Duffy to leave him alone. Or maybe he didn't understand what Duffy was saying."

"So what did they mean 'make her go away'?" Todd mused as his mother drove up.

"I don't know, but let's keep it to ourselves until we find out." Todd nodded.

THAT NIGHT, Gary sat in his room, staring at the handful of pills. Maybe Todd was right. He stared around the room at all his hockey posters of NHL superstars. His favourite players were mostly the smaller guys who had managed to make it in the league—guys like Theo Fleury and Wayne Gretzky. It's easy to make it when you're a big guy like Eric Lindros, his dad told him one time. The smaller players were all the more impressive because they made it on skill instead of size.

Gary wanted to believe that his dad was right. He rubbed his head gingerly. He'd taken a few hard hits in practice earlier, and his headaches had returned. He wasn't about to tell anyone, though. Dr. Champion would want him to sit out a couple of games for sure. With Todd back, the team was carrying an extra player. Someone would have to give up ice time. And even though he was among the team's top scorers, he just couldn't afford to miss any time.

Gary looked again at the pills. He knew lots of athletes took steroids, and he vaguely recalled a controversy about some baseball players. "They can't be that dangerous," he muttered to himself. "Otherwise none of those guys would take them either. Maybe they're only bad if you take too many." He thought again about Justin's ribbing in the locker room and made up his mind. He grabbed a pill and quickly downed it, swallowing a gulp of water to wash it down.

GARY FELT SICK to his stomach when he woke up the next morning. He had tossed and turned for most of the night. Every time he closed his eyes, he'd seen images of bulging muscles forcing their way out of his body and finally bursting.

"I took one," he confided to Todd as they sat in Mr. Doucette's English class during first period. Gary was pale and felt a cold sweat on his forehead. He wiped his brow, hoping his friend hadn't noticed.

"You're crazy," Todd whispered back. "Are you okay?"

Gary shook his head. A wave of nausea rose over him. He stumbled out the door and into the nearby washroom. He just barely made it into the cubicle before he threw up his breakfast.

Todd came running into the washroom, followed by Mr. Doucette.

"Are you okay?" the teacher asked. "I think we should take you down to the office."

Gary looked up at Todd and his teacher and shook his head. "No, I'm okay. Really. It must have been something I ate."

"But those pills…" Todd began. Gary glared at his friend, willing him to stop.

"I don't know what you're talking about," Gary said pointedly.

Mr. Doucette looked confused. "I'm afraid you're going to have to see someone about this, Gary. You can't just run out of class, throw up, and then pretend nothing happened."

"I'll go see my doctor. Right now," Gary suggested, looking for any way out of this mess. Todd nodded his encouragement.

The English teacher accepted Gary's compromise. "Take it easy, Gary. And be sure to check out at the office."

Todd gave Gary a stern look as he followed the teacher down the hallway back toward the classroom. Gary shrugged and reluctantly made his way to the principal's office.

Gary couldn't get in touch with his dad. At Mr. Bernard's insistence, he called his mother to come and pick him up.

"It's nothing, Mom," he said as he got into the car. "Mr. Doucette is just being super careful. I threw up. That's all."

"You don't just throw up for no reason. Is it the flu?" his mother inquired worriedly as they made their way toward the doctor's office a few blocks away. Gary shook his head.

"Is it the concussion coming back?" His mother was suddenly even more concerned.

"No, I'm fine," he replied. It felt good to have his mom worried about him again. Until very recently, she had been too busy to pay much attention to him or Maggie. This was more like the old days, when she was at home taking care of them.

"When are you going to come and stay at my place?" his mother asked, gently changing the subject.

"I'm so busy with hockey…" Gary said lamely. His mom looked disappointed, but she didn't push the issue any further.

When they reached Dr. Champion's office, Gary insisted that his mother drop him off and return to work. Reluctantly, she agreed. "Here. Take money for a taxi back to school or home. And call me at work to tell me what the doctor says."

Gary smiled at his mom as he closed the door. She rolled down the window. "And I want to hear from you more often, okay?" Gary felt puzzled as he watched his mom drive away. For months, he had nursed a grudge against her—after all, she was the one who had left them in the lurch. But he couldn't deny that his mom seemed happy with her new life. But where did his dad fit in? Gary still felt like he should take his dad's side, even if his mom was nice to him and still worried about him.

In the doctor's office, Gary stripped off his sweatshirt and waited nervously for Dr. Champion to arrive. He looked into his knapsack at the bag of pills. Even as he heard the doctor approach the door, he wasn't sure what he was going to tell her.

Dr. Champion asked him briefly about his symptoms. She checked his eyes and a worried look crossed her face.

"Are those headaches coming back?" she asked.

"No," Gary lied.

"So what made you throw up this morning?"

"I, uh, just had an upset stomach," Gary stuttered. The doctor wasn't buying his explanation. Gary suddenly realized that she was going to pin this whole episode on the concussion, and he was going to end up being benched! "If I tell you what the problem is, do you have to tell my parents?"

Dr. Champion looked confused. "What kind of problem are we talking about?"

"Never mind." Gary started pulling his sweatshirt back on.

"If it's the concussion, you should tell me. You shouldn't be playing hockey. Maybe we should schedule some X-rays."

Gary shook his head.

"Gary, tell me what's wrong. I can't help you if you won't tell me."

"And my parents?"

"Unless you're breaking the law or in some kind of danger, I don't have to tell them," Dr. Champion explained.

Gary paused for a moment. He felt another wave of nausea as he thought about taking the pill. He reached into his knapsack and tentatively handed Dr. Champion the plastic bag. He watched as she sifted through the contents, examining some of the pills closely.

"Gary, do you realize what these are?"

He shook his head. "I don't know exactly. Some guy on my team gave them to me. I only took one," he added quickly.

The doctor shook her head. "I don't know what this guy was trying to pull on you, but this is heavy stuff. Most of the pills in here are anabolic steroids. If I'm remembering what I've read in medical journals correctly, these are the same ones used on cattle. You can't even get them legally in Canada," Dr. Champion explained. "Then there's some Sudafed. That's a decongestant. And there's another one, too. I don't know the brand name, but I'm pretty sure it's used for horses."

Gary felt sick to his stomach again.

"Which one is that?" he asked weakly.

"It doesn't matter which one you took. They're all bad for you," his doctor reprimanded him. "Who gave these to you?"

Gary didn't answer.

"Oh, is this some kind of code of silence thing? Well this kid, whoever he is, is breaking the law for one thing. And putting his health at risk. I need to know who it is," Dr. Champion insisted.

Gary just shook his head. "Am I going to be okay?"

Exasperated, the doctor tossed her stethoscope onto the counter and washed her hands. "*If* you stay away from this stuff. I'm serious, Gary. This is dangerous business, especially the stuff for horses and cattle."

"Is that what made me sick?" he asked.

Dr. Champion shook her head. "No, one pill probably wouldn't have had that dramatic an effect. I think you were probably so stressed out that you made yourself throw up. Or your body was smart enough to get that stuff out of your system. Whatever it was, I'm hanging on to these pills."

As Gary jumped down off the examination table, Dr. Champion turned to him. "Gary, I'm going to have to tell your parents about this."

"You said you didn't have to!" Gary exclaimed. "You promised."

"Not if what you're doing is illegal! These pills could seriously harm somebody if taken in the wrong combination," Dr. Champion explained. "I have to tell your parents. Be thankful I'm not going to the police."

"Okay, how about if I tell them? Is that good enough?"

"Have them give me a call," his doctor insisted. "And if I don't hear from them, you can expect a call from me. Got it?"

Gary nodded.

"And I need you to do something else for me." Dr. Champion held up the bag of pills in her hand. "You tell whoever gave these to you to smarten up or he's going to get himself into some serious health trouble."

On his way back to school, Gary felt both relieved and confused. What was he going to tell Todd? Or his parents? Worst of all, what was he going to say to Justin? He wanted to keep his promise to the doctor, but he knew it wasn't going to be easy.

 **ANOTHER BLOW**

GARY ARRIVED BACK at school just in time for lunch. He scanned the cafeteria looking for Todd. As he made his way over to his friend's table, he bumped into Justin.

"Hey, MacWuss," Justin said in a teasing voice. "How's the tummy? I hear you had a little bonding session with the toilet bowl this morning."

Justin's friends burst into laughter and Gary felt his face turning red.

"What's the matter, MacWuss?" Justin continued. "Didn't have your oatmeal or something? Or did you take your vitamins on an empty stomach?"

Gary had had enough. "Well, at least I'm not going to start mooing because of some stupid cattle pills," he said sarcastically. "Or was it a horse pill today? Feel like some hay for lunch?"

The instant the words were out of his mouth, Gary regretted them.

"I don't know what you're talking about," Justin said. "Do you have a problem with my, um, vitamin supplements?"

"Never mind, Justin," Todd said, stepping to Gary's defence. He had obviously heard the last part of Gary's statement. "Let's go, Gar."

"No, I want to hear what he has to say," Justin insisted. "Tell me more, MacWuss."

Gary took a deep breath. "It's just…my doctor…she says those pills you gave me are for cows and horses."

Justin glared back. "You are so gullible, MacWuss. Do you believe everything your doctor tells you? She's just trying to keep you from growing any real muscle on that wimpy body of yours. Grow up."

"Man, oh man. Not only are you a weakling, you're gullible too," snorted Tony, another of Justin's friends.

"Mooo, mooo," Mike Bartlett joined in. The boys laughed and walked away, making cow and horse noises as they crossed the cafeteria.

Gary followed Todd to a nearby table and sank into a seat. He noticed some of the kids looking at him and laughing. He could still hear Justin and the others making animal sounds.

"So, the pills are bad for you?" Todd asked.

"Yeah. They're not for people, they're for animals," Gary replied. He was too embarrassed to tell his friend that it was his nerves and not the pills that had made him sick. Gary felt the throbbing start in his temples. Last night's headache was coming back.

"What are you going to do?" Todd inquired.

Gary shrugged. "Well, Justin obviously doesn't care. The doctor said I should tell him because they could make him sick. Now he's just going to moo at me for the rest of the season."

"Where are the pills now?"

"I had to give them to my doctor. And she said I had to tell my parents, or she was going to call them," Gary explained.

"The police?"

"Those pills are illegal. I don't know where Justin got them. But he could get in big trouble."

"What do you think your dad is going to say?"

Gary shuddered. "I don't know. I just hope he doesn't make a big deal out of it."

LATER THAT NIGHT, his father came into his room. Donny had missed supper again. Gary was surprised to see his father wearing jeans and a sweater. He had assumed that his dad was working late.

"Maggie tells me that you were sick at school today," Donny said, settling onto the bed.

"It was no big deal. I just took some vitamins. On an empty stomach," Gary explained.

"What vitamins?" his father asked. He was only half listening as he flipped through a Snow Dogs magazine that Gary had next to his bed.

Gary was desperately trying to think of some way to avoid telling his dad about the steroids. He remembered Dr. Champion's threat. It would be much worse coming from her. He took a deep breath.

"Vitamins someone gave me," Gary muttered. He looked over at his father. "Actually, they were steroids. Dr. Champion says they're for cows and horses. So I guess I was pretty dumb to take them."

Donny put down the magazine and turned to face Gary. Anger flashed across his face. "Why would you do something like that?" he demanded. "Who gave the pills to you? I want a name!"

Gary shrugged his shoulders. "I was just tired of being so small. I'm never going to make it—"

"Haven't we had this conversation before?" his father interrupted. "You don't get anywhere in this world by cheating or muscling your way around. It takes hard work and some talent. You're willing to work hard, and you've got talent. Be thankful."

"But everyone is bigger than me!" Gary said, trying not to whine.

"Tough," his father replied. "Horse steroids are not going to make the difference. You're lucky you only got sick to your stomach! It could have been a lot worse."

The doorbell rang downstairs. His father stood up quickly. Gary looked at his watch: nine o'clock. Who was coming over so late?

"I've got to go," his father said. "But no more pills. If I catch you pulling something like this again, you're out of hockey. Am I clear?" Gary nodded silently, but his father wasn't done. "When I get home, you're going to tell me who gave you those pills. Got it?"

His father closed the door firmly behind him, not even allowing Gary to respond. He stared at the wall, wondering what was going to happen to his family next. As if on cue, his head started to ache. Just what he needed.

Gary thought about what his father had said. He could tell his dad was serious when he threatened to take him out of hockey. Gary had rarely seen his father so angry. Maybe he was lucky the doorbell had rung. He was too distracted now to even care where his father had gone.

The light was making his head hurt even more. Gary turned it off and lay in the darkness. It took him hours to fall asleep, but he didn't hear his dad come back. And there was still no sign of him when Gary and Maggie got up the next morning and left for school.

THE NEXT DAY in the dressing room before the game, Justin pointedly ignored Gary. "Hey, Manning." Justin spoke to Todd, but he glared at Gary as he talked. "I bet you're moving up to the first line someday soon."

"Yeah, Gary and I can't wait to be on the same line again," Todd sniped back. "Too bad you'll be dropped down, but I guess them's the breaks."

Justin scowled. "I'd watch my back if I were you." Before Todd could respond, Coach Mulligan walked into the dressing room.

"Manning, I want you up on the first line. MacDonald, you move to left wing, Bartlett on the right. Johnston, you're with MacLean and Docherty. Questions?"

Gary smiled but didn't dare look in Justin's direction. He knew the older boy was fuming. It was just as Todd had predicted. Finally, he and Todd were back together. As Gary skated out onto the ice, he looked up in the stands. He immediately spotted his father. Then he noticed his mother sitting in another area of the bleachers. He gave her a quick wave, and wondered if she, too, had spotted Donny.

It felt good having Todd back on his line, and the two friends dominated the Abbies' offence. Gary scored once, Mike Bartlett once, and Todd had assists on both. However, by the third period, the team was down 3–2, and Gary was starting to feel frustrated. The Sherwood defencemen were all over him every time he got into their zone. Coach

Mulligan was yelling at him to get out in front of the net, but the bigger players kept grabbing him. "Hey, they're holding," Gary protested to the nearby linesman, but the man only shrugged. Gary fumed on the bench, determined to shake off the defencemen during the next shift.

On the next play, Todd and Gary skated down the ice, deftly passing the puck through the neutral zone and toward the net. Gary pulled away from the Sherwood defender, giving him an elbow as he skated past. He then gave the player a hard poke with his stick as he headed behind the net. The ref blew his whistle.

"Slashing, number 87," he shouted and directed Gary to the penalty box.

"Oh great," Gary muttered as he skated to the penalty box. Coach Mulligan shot him a furious look from across the ice. "I get called and they get away with holding every time," Gary snapped at the ref.

"You want another two?" the ref threatened. "'Cause I'll give 'em to ya." Gary didn't answer.

Todd skated over to the penalty box. "Coach says for you and Justin to switch next shift," Todd said guiltily. "Sorry," he added.

The two minutes seemed to drag on forever. Gary was in a foul mood by the time he reached the Abbies' bench. The next shift, he jumped on the ice with the second line. He headed down to the Sherwood zone, determined to get his revenge. He pushed his way in front of the net, waiting for a pass. Suddenly, he felt a shove from behind and his legs flew out from under him. He landed on the ice in a heap. His head was the last to hit.

Gary opened his eyes to see the Abbies' trainer bent over him. "We're taking you to Emergency," he said, slowly helping Gary to his feet. Gary saw his mother and father standing together by the boards. Then everything went black.

THEY WAITED FOR HOURS in the emergency department. Gary's mom and dad didn't say much to each other, but having both of them there made him feel better somehow. Eventually Gary was sent for X-rays and then put on a table in one of the examining rooms. As he lay there, he could hear his mother asking his father what he was going to do about getting Gary off the Abbies. Gary strained to hear his dad's answer, but he couldn't make it out. He could tell from their voices that they were on the verge of arguing.

A little later, the doctor returned. Gary had suffered a concussion, more severe than his first head injury.

"They start to have a cumulative effect," the doctor explained, writing out a prescription for some pain medication. "You're going to have to think long and hard about how much you want to keep playing hockey."

Gary's head was aching too much to even consider debating with the doctor. He noticed his mother and father listening carefully. He was going to have a hard time convincing them to let him play this weekend. He slowly sat up and started getting dressed, determined not to let his parents see how much his head was hurting.

"Let's go home," he muttered.

WHO'S A WIMP NOW? 10

GARY'S HEAD WAS still aching the next morning. When he finally went downstairs for breakfast, he was surprised to see his mother sitting at the table.

"Well, your hockey days are over for a while," his mother said, rushing over to help him sit down. "I don't know why they have kids your age hitting in the first place."

Gary wanted to protest, but his mouth felt like it was full of marbles. "Where's Dad?"

"Just back from the drugstore," his father said, walking in the door. "You're supposed to take it easy for a couple of days," he turned to face his wife. "Should he even be out of bed?" Martha looked worried but shrugged her shoulders. "Can I get you some breakfast?"

"Nah, I'm not hungry," Gary replied. Then he realized that his mother and father were together in the house again—for the first time since his mother had left. It seemed weird to have his mom back in their kitchen.

"Okay, maybe I'll have some toast. And eggs," Gary suggested.

"I'll drop by the school and pick up your homework," Gary's dad told him, heading toward the door. "Thanks for coming over," he said politely to Martha. She nodded. "And you really don't mind about the furniture?"

Donny shook his head. "No, take whatever you need. The kids and I will move stuff around later."

Gary watched with curiosity as his father headed out the door. "What furniture?"

"Oh, I'm moving to a bigger apartment in the same building," his mom explained. "It has a great view of the harbour and three bedrooms. So I needed some more furniture. Your dad agreed to let me take some of the extra stuff from here."

Gary was disappointed. He'd been so pleased to see his parents talking civilly again, at least for part of the time. And now this. His mom was just here to pick up some furniture. He picked up the newspaper, hoping she wouldn't notice the tears welling up in his eyes.

Gary scanned the front page of the *Guardian*. A caption at the top of the page caught his eye: "Russian star takes a beating." He quickly flipped to the sports section, heart pounding. There was a large photo of Dmitri in the middle of a brawl. It had happened last night in Albany. The report said that Dmitri had been caught in the middle of a bench-clearing brawl that started when one of the River Rats pushed the young Russian into the net. Duffy had responded, throwing the River Rats player into the boards. Both teams had quickly poured onto the ice and paired up in individual fights.

"Look at this," Gary waved the paper at Maggie, who had just appeared in the kitchen. "Dmitri was in a big fight. He has a bunch of stitches."

"Who's Dmitri?" his mother asked, giving Maggie a hug.

"What happened?" Maggie asked, grabbing the paper from her brother. "No way!"

"How do you two know this guy?" his mother asked curiously.

"Dmitri Rushkov," Gary explained. "He's a Russian player with the Snow Dogs. He's our friend. He comes over and watches hockey and eats pizza with us. He's lonely."

"I guess it would be a big change coming here from Russia. How's his English?" Martha inquired.

"Not bad," Maggie replied. "So he got into a big fight, eh? I bet Duffy stood up for him—only to make himself look good, I'm sure."

"What do you have against Duffy?" Gary asked.

"Some kids at school are saying Duffy got one of the Grade 12 girls pregnant," Maggie explained. "Now the team is going to trade him, just to get him out of town."

Gary stared at his sister in shock. He didn't want to believe what she was saying, but it made sense. That must have been what Clark Dinsmore was talking about. He had told Cheryl Porter to "take care of it."

"What happened to the girl?" Gary asked.

"She's dropped out. None of her friends know where she is and her parents aren't saying. Rumour is she's gone to Halifax."

Gary's mom looked at her daughter with concern. "I don't like the sound of this. *You* aren't hanging around with these guys, are you?"

Gary piped up. "Mom, Dmitri isn't like that—"

Maggie interrupted him before he could finish. "I can take care of myself," she insisted. "And Gary's right. Dmitri's not like the rest of those jerks. And the word is out now that these guys are pigs. Anyone with brains will stay away from them. The puck bunnies probably still hang around, but who cares what happens to them."

"Maggie, that's not very nice," her mother reprimanded her. "I'm sure the girls are just, well, misdirected. It must seem glamorous dating a hockey player."

"Mom, these guys don't date. They just use women and dump them," Maggie corrected her mother. "But the girls say that Dmitri wasn't even interested in talking to them, never mind anything else."

Gary looked at his sister in surprise. She met his gaze. "You were right, okay?"

"Alright, alright," her mother waved her hands in the air. "Just stay out of trouble. As for you, take care of that head of yours." She gave Gary a light kiss on the top of his head. "No more hockey until you're totally recovered. And Dr. Champion wants you to drop by when you're feeling better."

GARY SLEPT THE REST of the morning. The house was quiet without Maggie and his dad around. But by early afternoon, the novelty of a day away from school was starting to wear off. He was bored. Although he was still a bit woozy, his head *was* feeling better, and he was anxious to get out of the house. He decided to take a walk. Automatically, he headed down toward the Civic Centre.

It was a crisp late autumn day and the fallen red and orange maple leaves skipped across the sidewalk. As he drew closer to the rink, he saw the big Snow Dogs' bus making the turn off St. Peter's Road. The team was back. Gary walked faster, tucking his hands in his pockets to keep them warm in the brisk November wind.

By the time he reached the Civic Centre, the bus had been emptied and the equipment was piled outside the Snow Dogs' dressing room. Gary snuck in through a back door propped open with a broomstick. He almost bumped into Gunner.

"Hey kid, haven't seen you for a while," the old trainer said gruffly. "You looking for Dmitri?"

Gary nodded. "Is he still around?"

"He's here somewhere. He had to head to the team doctor to get those stitches checked out. His face is a mess." The older man shook his head in disgust. "Those goons really worked him over."

"Why were they picking on him?" Gary asked, worried about his friend.

"It's probably because he's Russian. The big guys can't stand looking stupid next to these speedy Europeans. You know how that hothead on TV goes on and on about the Europeans? What's his name? Bobby Dawson. You know the guy. He's always mouthing off about Russians being wimps. Well, this is what happens," Gunner explained.

"I don't get it," Gary persisted. "They went after Dmitri just because he's from Russia?"

"He wears one of those face guards, right? Well, the goons think that makes him easy pickin'. Europeans don't fight, right?" Gunner tossed a broken stick into the garbage can with such force that the whole can shook. "The coaches tell these guys to slow down the best players. And this is how they do it. They nag away at them. Tease them about the face guards. Jab them here and there. And sometimes it gets messy. Like the game in Albany."

"Well, can't the Snow Dogs do anything about it?" Gary asked, hoping he didn't sound stupid.

"Yeah, that's what players like Duffy and Sanders are there for. To protect the high-priced talent. But sometimes they get in there too late. And sometimes, well, you have to toughen guys like Dmitri up. After all, it's not going to get any better in the big league," Gunner concluded.

Gary had lots more questions, but the old trainer had turned his attention to a batch of skates that needed sharpening. Just then, Dmitri came around the corner. His face lit up when he saw Gary. The young Russian pointed to his stitches and shrugged.

"You like my new look? I have a few problems shaving," Dmitri joked.

"Does it hurt?" Gary asked, staring at the three sets of stitches that now dominated Dmitri's face.

"No, not so much," Dmitri replied. "They were big goons. But they don't scare me. After all, I am so much faster. Next time, they don't catch me. I know them now."

"That doesn't seem fair," Gary replied. "I mean, they're just going to get away with this?"

Dmitri shrugged. "It is part of the game. It is the price I pay for being small and fast. They know I will be in the NHL someday. And they will only be tough guys in the small towns. I think that makes them mad."

Gary wasn't convinced, but he didn't say anything more. He was trying to figure out a way to ask Dmitri about Duffy when Coach Mulligan came around the corner.

"MacDonald, what are you doing here? Last I heard, you were in the hospital."

"No, just home from school. I'm supposed to be resting, I guess," Gary admitted meekly. "I, uh, just, uh, needed to look for a shirt I left here. After the game. I mean, because I left the game."

Dmitri eyed Gary with concern. "Why were you at the hospital?"

Coach Mulligan looked more than a little surprised. He glanced from Dmitri to Gary, and back again. "You know this guy?" he asked the Russian.

"Yes, I am friends with him and his family. They have been very kind to me. They give me pizza and *Hockey Night in Canada*," Dmitri smiled and then grimaced. He gingerly touched the stitches on his cheek.

"You get home," the Coach commanded, turning his attention back to Gary. "And don't come back until that head of yours is better." The Coach strode off toward the dressing room, tapping his clipboard against the concrete wall.

"I have a concussion." Gary said reluctantly.

"What does this mean, 'concussion'?" Dmitri asked.

"You know, I hurt my head. I get bad headaches. If I get another one, I might have to quit hockey," Gary explained. He thought about what the emergency room doctor had said. He knew Dr. Champion would not hesitate to keep him out of hockey if his head didn't get better—maybe even for good. Gary shuddered. He had always played hockey. He couldn't imagine not coming back ever again.

"I have heard of such stories in Russia, too," Dmitri replied seriously. "I am very sorry to hear this. But you will play hockey again, no?"

Gary felt his chin start to tremble. "I guess so."

"When you do, I will help you get back in shape," Dmitri proposed.

Suddenly, from down the corridor, Gary and Dmitri could hear the sound of raised voices. Then a slamming door. Rob Duffy came striding down the hallway.

He walked up to Dmitri and shoved him hard. "Thanks a lot, you traitor," Duffy shouted. Dmitri looked shocked. Gary quickly moved out of the way as Duffy grabbed Dmitri's shirt and pushed him up against the wall.

"What did you tell them, you little Russian snitch? I try to be friends with you and this is what I get? Suspended by the league for doing my job! Then I find out I'm traded because some local girl says I got her in trouble. Did you tell them?" Dmitri was still pinned to the wall and Duffy was almost spitting as he screamed into the Russian player's face.

Gunner came rushing up and separated the two. "You little pipsqueak," he planted both hands firmly on Duffy's chest and gave a good hard push. The player stumbled backward, away from Dmitri. "You've got nerve, picking on this kid. He's not the one who can't keep his pants zipped. And as for the suspension…that's your job. To take a fall for the stars of the team. Get used to it or get out!" Now Gunner was as angry as Duffy. His face had turned bright red and he was shaking his fist at the young player.

Just then, Dave Anderson arrived on the scene. "Enough, Gunner. Calm down. Your heart…" the Coach said softly. He turned to face Duffy. "You, out of here. And you'd better hope our paths don't cross again. I don't need the likes of you on my team."

Rob Duffy picked up his hockey bag and threw it over his shoulder. "My pleasure. I can't wait to get out of this two-bit town. Bunch of potato farmers and their sleazy daughters…" He looked like he wanted to say more but Gunner stopped him with another lunge.

"Whoa, Gunner. He's not worth it," Anderson repeated. "Rushky, you okay?" Dmitri nodded. The Coach gave Gary a quick look and then turned back to his star. "How're the stitches? You gonna be able to play tomorrow."

"I must keep on my face visor," Dmitri said, breaking into a slow grin. "Even if it means I am, how you say, a wimp."

Dave Anderson gave a loud guffaw. "Hey, I was one of the toughest guys around. And if I could do it over again, I'd wear one of those contraptions, too. Instead I've got all these beauty marks." He rubbed his face where a prominent scar zigzagged from his cheekbone down to the corner of his mouth. "Mind you, the doctors are a little more talented today. I'm sure your face will be good as new when they're finished with you."

Dmitri looked relieved. The Coach slapped him on the back and headed toward the dressing room. Just before he rounded the corner, he turned back. "And Gunner—next time, let me handle the goons."

Gunner grinned and then nodded goodbye to Dmitri and Gary.

"So, pizza tonight? My treat, your house," Dmitri said brightly, trying to change the mood.

Gary was about to agree. Then he remembered Maggie.

"Dmitri," he said tentatively. "Maggie says she saw you and Duffy at the bar."

"Oh, I did not see her. I am sorry," Dmitri seemed sincere.

"She, uh, says that you and Duffy invited a bunch of girls back to your apartment," Gary continued. He had to know the truth, especially after the scene with Duffy.

"Duffy wanted to have a party. I did not understand," Dmitri explained. "When so many girls came to my apartment, I said they must go home. They were so young girls. Duffy was mad with me. They go to his apartment instead. I go to sleep."

Gary sighed with relief.

"Why you ask me about this?" Dmitri inquired.

"Well, Maggie was sort of mad," Gary answered, choosing his words carefully.

"Because why?" Dmitri continued.

"Because she thought you were taking advantage of those girls," Gary blurted out. "She said you were just another hot-shot player, thinking he could have any girl he wanted."

Dmitri looked puzzled. "But I am not like Duffy. I have girl-friend. In Russia. I not look for girlfriend in Canada."

Gary was surprised. Dmitri had talked a lot about his mother and Pavel, but he'd never mentioned a girlfriend. Dmitri seemed to sense his surprise.

"Come, I give you ride home," Dmitri suggested.

They went out to the parking lot. Dmitri pointed toward a grey Ford truck. He dangled the keys with pleasure. "It is mine," he said proudly. "My first truck."

Gary almost laughed out loud. The truck was a couple of years old, and easily the smallest one in the lot. Even the cleaning staff at the rink had bigger and better vehicles.

"It's nice, Dmitri. But why didn't you get a new one?" Gary asked politely as they climbed in.

Dmitri shook his head. "I need to send my money back to Russia, to my mother and Pavel. And I save money to bring my girlfriend to Canada." He shyly pulled a picture out of his wallet and showed it to Gary. "Her name is Tatiana and she is very beautiful. She is schoolteacher. She learns English to come to Canada and be teacher here, too. Maybe we get married next year."

Gary was amazed to see Dmitri blush. The Russian player seemed awfully young to be getting married, at least Gary thought so. He couldn't imagine his sister being that serious with anyone, and she was only two years younger than Dmitri. Still, Gary reasoned, Dmitri had obviously grown up a lot faster, having to leave Russia and come to a strange country. Dmitri carefully pulled the truck up in front of the MacDonalds' house.

"My parents are getting divorced," Gary said suddenly. He wasn't sure what prompted him to say this. Maybe it was just an afternoon for explaining stuff.

"I am sorry," Dmitri replied. "Your mother. She lives here in Charlottetown?"

Gary realized he'd never even mentioned his mother to Dmitri. He felt guilty, remembering how worried his mother had been this morning. "Yes, in an apartment downtown. Maybe you can meet her some time." Gary suggested as he got out of the truck. Dmitri smiled. "So, 7:30 for pizza?"

"Your sister will not be mad at me?" Dmitri asked earnestly.

"Nah, she didn't really think you were like that anyway," he replied.

Gary had a smile on his face as Dmitri pulled away. He

couldn't wait to tell Maggie everything that had happened this afternoon. Duffy was traded and Dmitri had a girlfriend. This would have been a really great day, Gary thought as he went up to his room and lay down—if only his head didn't ache so much.

HEAD GAMES 11

GARY COULDN'T BELIEVE it was almost Christmas. His thirteenth birthday had come and gone and, at long last, the MacDonald rink was ready. Now he and Dmitri were in the backyard, putting up the nets at opposite ends. The boards were up, with team benches on either side. Donny had even painted lines on the ice and strung up lights so Gary and his friends could play well into the evening. Dmitri had been amazed at the elaborate preparations.

"In Russia, we have not so many rinks as in Canada. Only the best players get to use them. Our arenas are very cold and the ice is not so smooth as here in your yard," Dmitri teased.

"But I bet this is the first time you've had to stand with a hose and water down the ice," Gary replied with a grin.

"This is true," Dmitri rubbed his hands together to warm them up. "So now, we are ready to start your training."

"I've been doing some weights and sit-ups and stuff," Gary said enthusiastically. His headaches had stopped, but Dr. Champion still had not given him the green light to go back to full-contact hockey. At least he was allowed to skate with the team again, as long as he avoided any checking.

The Abbies were doing well and were currently tied with their arch-rivals from Parkdale. Todd was leading the league in scoring and Justin had returned full-time to the first line. Gary went to all the games in Charlottetown, but he was finding it hard to watch. He felt like everyone on the team had forgotten him, especially Coach Mulligan.

Dmitri, meanwhile, had healed as well. The scars were hardly noticeable, though Dmitri continued to wear his full face visor. Darby Sanders was now assigned to protect Dmitri if any of the opposing players started to get on his back.

No one mentioned Rob Duffy anymore. He had been traded to the International Hockey League, so the Snow Dogs didn't have to worry about playing against their former teammate. And the girl from Maggie's school was back. No one knew for sure what had happened to her, but she told her friends that she'd been paid by the Snow Dogs not to talk about her relationship with Rob Duffy.

"Let's play some shinny," Gary suggested to Dmitri.

"What is this, 'shinny'?" Dmitri asked.

"You know, pickup hockey," Gary explained.

"Like pickup truck?" Dmitri smiled.

"Yeah, right," Gary chuckled. "Wow, Dmitri. You can even make jokes in English now."

"What's the joke?" Donny MacDonald asked, as he walked up to the rink. There was a woman with him, and she gave Dmitri and Gary a friendly smile. Gary looked away.

"Uh, Dmitri said 'pickup truck' instead of 'pickup hockey,'" Gary mumbled.

"Lisa, this is my son, Gary." He ruffled Gary's hair playfully, making him feel even more self-conscious. "And this is Dmitri

Rushkov. He plays for the Charlottetown Snow Dogs and has become a regular at our supper table. Pizza with the works for this guy!"

"Hi, I'm Lisa McCulloch. I work with Donny. I mean, your dad," Lisa said with a quick laugh.

Though Gary wanted to dislike Lisa, he had to admit that she was good-looking. She was blonde and athletic, in jeans, sneakers, and a down-filled vest.

"You've done a marvellous job on the rink, Gary," Lisa said with a smile. "And Dmitri. Of course, I've been following your progress with the Snow Dogs. How are you enjoying Charlottetown?"

"Very much, thank you," said Dmitri. "The MacDonalds have been very kind to me. We eat much pizza together."

They all laughed, except Gary.

"We play pickup hockey now," Dmitri said, grabbing one of the many sticks he had given Gary. He handed one to Donny and then turned to Lisa. "You would like one, too? I know that North American girls, like Maggie, play hockey. It is something new I learn since I came to Canada."

"Sure, I'd love to play," Lisa smiled, giving Donny a pleased look. "I'm not much good, but I'll give it a shot."

"Okay, Lisa and me against Dmitri and Gary," Donny suggested.

"Uh, I think I'd better pass," Gary said suddenly. "I've got a bit of a headache."

"I thought your head was better," Donny said with concern in his voice.

"Well, I guess it's not," Gary snapped. "You go ahead without me." He stormed into the house and slammed the door. A few minutes later, he heard Dmitri knock softly. The Russian slowly opened the door and came in. He sat down at the kitchen table across from Gary.

"I think it's not your head that hurts so much," Dmitri said quietly. Gary poured Dmitri a mug of hot chocolate and sat down at the table.

"Why does everything have to change?" Gary grumbled. "I miss my mom. I want *her* back, not some woman from Dad's office! Oh, I don't even know who to be mad at anymore. Everyone, I guess."

"I never knew my father," Dmitri told Gary. "I think you are very lucky to have two such good parents, even if they don't live together. Someday you will know this, too."

"I guess so," Gary nodded his head forlornly. "But it still hurts."

Dmitri was silent for a while. "I will miss you MacDonalds when I go to New Mexico," the hockey player said finally.

"You're going up?" Gary asked in a surprised voice.

Dmitri shrugged his shoulders. "Gunner says that the Coach thinks I am almost ready. Coach wanted me to have some fights, like in Albany. He wants me to be tougher, ready for the big NHL."

"That will be really cool," Gary said, his voice perking up with excitement. Dmitri's response was less enthusiastic. "It is my dream, yes, but it will also be hard. There is so much to think about. So much pressures. Reporters. Big star players. Coaches who must win to keep their jobs. Sometimes I miss hockey, like here. Pickup hockey."

Gary got up from the table and started pulling his jacket back on. "Let's go play some pickup, then," he said cheerfully. "My head's feeling much better."

As they walked out the door, Gary stopped in his tracks. His dad and Lisa were standing on the rink, with their arms around each other. He turned around to go back in the house and almost crashed into Dmitri. Then he changed his mind. He stormed over to the rink.

"Okay, we need the ice now," Gary said, not meeting his father's eyes.

"Same teams?" Donny said playfully, giving Lisa a squeeze.

"No teams," Gary replied. "I need to work on my game. I don't have time for fooling around." He gave his father a pointed look.

"Gary, we can do some shooting later," Dmitri suggested.

"No, I want to do it now," Gary insisted.

"You don't have to be rude," his father reprimanded him. "The rink is here for everyone."

"It's not here to add to your social life," Gary shot back. "I think only serious hockey players should be allowed here."

Donny turned to Lisa with a pained look on his face. "I'm sorry about this..."

"No, Gary's right," Lisa said, trying to be cheerful. "It's important that he gets back in shape for hockey. After all, the Abbies need him back in the lineup."

"No, actually, they don't," Gary shouted. "They're doing just fine without me. Thanks for reminding me."

Now everyone looked embarrassed. Gary went to the garage and grabbed a bag of pucks. He came storming back and threw them onto the ice. He started taking shots at the net and almost hit Lisa in the head with one.

"Let's get going," Donny spoke to his date, but his eyes were fixed on Gary. "I'll deal with you later." Gary just stared back at him defiantly. He watched as his dad and Lisa walked to her car and climbed in. They had what looked like an animated discussion and, finally, they drove away.

"Now I'm in for it," Gary said to Dmitri, who had been quiet throughout the entire scene.

"You are wrong about the Abbies," Dmitri told him, flipping a puck in Gary's direction. "They miss you, I am sure."

"But I'm too small," Gary replied. "And if I get one more concussion, I'm finished."

"You can't think like that or it will come true," Dmitri advised. "You must remember why you play. For moments like this."

The Russian made a quick move around Gary and scored a pretty goal. He raised his hands in triumph and grinned like a little kid. Before Dmitri could get set, Gary slipped by him and headed toward the opposite net. Gary could hear the Russian turning and skating to catch up. But just as Dmitri slipped past and reached for the puck, Gary deked the other way and went around him.

"He shoots, he scores!" Gary shouted.

Dmitri skated up and gave Gary a high-five.

"He shoots, he scores!" Dmitri echoed in his thick Russian accent.

After Dmitri left, Gary replayed the moment over and over in his mind. It had been magical—like something straight out of The Dream. Gary wished his father could have been there to see his goal against a future NHL star. Now that some time had passed, he was feeling bad about the way he'd treated Lisa. After all, it wasn't her fault his parents were splitting up. He hoped his dad would forgive him. The back-

yard rink was a special place, and he'd used it to make someone feel unwanted. He made himself a promise to never do
that again. The rink was about just two things: playing the
game and having fun.

12 COACH'S CHOICE

GARY MANAGED TO AVOID his dad for the rest of the weekend. And on Monday at his checkup with Dr. Champion, he finally got a piece of good news. She agreed to let him rejoin the Abbies' lineup, on the condition that he'd head to the bench, instantly, if his headaches returned. Gary should have been thrilled, but the scene with his father was still bothering him. Reluctantly, he called his father at work to ask for a ride to the game.

"Sure," Donny said, though his voice was cool. "I'll see you at home around suppertime."

They drove to the rink in silence. Gary wanted to apologize for his behaviour toward Lisa, but he wasn't quite sure what to say. His dad, meanwhile, stared straight ahead and didn't even try to strike up a conversation.

"Can you come back and pick me up?" Gary asked tentatively as he hauled his hockey gear out of the back. He was surprised that his dad had pulled into a parking spot and stopped the van. He had assumed that his father would just head back home.

"Actually, I'd like to watch," Donny replied, still not making eye contact with his son. They headed in opposite directions as soon as they entered the Civic Centre, Donny to the stands and Gary to the Abbies' dressing room.

Coach Mulligan looked surprised to see Gary. "You back in the lineup, kid?" he asked, consulting his clipboard.

"Yeah, Dr. Champion said I could play now, hits and all," Gary said, a pleased smile on his face. He gazed around the dressing room in contentment, breathing in the familiar smell of dried sweat and soggy leather. In the background, the loud beat of music from the CD player competed with the raucous laughter of his teammates getting ready for the game.

"We don't need you today, MacDonald," Coach Mulligan said abruptly. "We're sending you down to AA."

Gary stared at him in disbelief. "You can't do that. I'm better now," he sputtered.

"The paperwork is done," the Coach said, with a tone of finality in his voice. "Give it some time, kid. You need...some time." He turned his back on Gary and started to walk away.

"But I was the top scorer in the league," Gary argued. His voice was shaking slightly, but it grew louder as he felt the full force of his rejection. "I'm better. I'm ready to play."

The Coach just shook his head and left the room. The rest of the team was silent now—only the loud music blared away obnoxiously. Gary walked over and angrily turned it off. Then he picked up his equipment bag and stormed out of the dressing room.

Todd came rushing after him. "Gary, wait. You have to go talk to the Coach. It's a mistake. He's got to let you play."

Gary turned to his friend in a fury. "Didn't you hear him? It's over. I'm in AA," he snarled. Then he paused. "No, actually. I quit."

"What's going on?" Donny MacDonald asked, coming out of the men's washroom and into the hallway.

"I've been sent down," Gary said, his voice filled with anger. "I'm not good enough for the Abbies anymore. So…I quit."

Gary's dad turned to Todd. "Is this true?"

Todd nodded.

"You boys wait here," Donny snapped, storming toward the dressing room. Gary tried to grab his father's arm as he reached the dressing room door, but Donny pushed him away. Inside the room, Coach Mulligan looked up in surprise at the intrusion.

"Let's step outside," Coach Mulligan suggested, sensing the nature of Donny's visit.

"No, let's have it out right here," Donny replied, his legs astride, as if challenging the Coach to a bout.

"Donny, I had to do it. The kid's just too vulnerable. It's for his own good," Coach Mulligan said in a low voice, pulling Gary's dad to one corner of the dressing room. All the boys strained forward, hoping to hear what the Coach was saying. Gary tried to avoid their eyes, not wanting to see the pity in their faces. He was partly embarrassed by his father's behaviour. But another of part of him was thrilled to see his dad coming to his defence—even if it was too late.

"For his own good? No, keeping the goons from the other teams away from him, that would have been for his own good," Donny corrected the Coach. He picked up a stick and waved it for emphasis. "Cleaning up the cheap shots by the other team would have helped. And keeping damn checking out of hockey would have been for his own good. But sending him down to AA sure as hell is not."

"Checking is part of the game," the Coach said defensively. "If he can't take it, he shouldn't be up with the big team."

"Vince, do you hear yourself? These are kids, dammit! This is not the NHL. It's supposed to be about fun, not about who can slam whom into the boards. How did it get to be so damn serious?" Donny fumed. Then, as suddenly as he had appeared in the dressing room, Donny disappeared out the door. Gary looked at the Coach, who stood suddenly silent in the centre of the room.

"Get dressed, kid," he mumbled, waving at Gary. He glanced around the room at the rest of the players. "And you twerps, mind your own business. We've got a game to play. Get dressed."

Gary got into his gear in silence. He snuck a look around the room every once in a while, but no one was saying much and everyone was careful to avoid his glance. He could hear the Coach in the other room, chewing out one of the assistants.

"Undo the damn paperwork," the Coach snapped. "I don't care who you have to phone or how many times. Get him back on the team. And I don't want to hear another word about it."

As the team headed out onto the ice, Gary took a look at the stands. His dad was standing at the glass, his hands scrunched into his pockets. He gave Gary a tense grimace as his son skated out onto the ice. One of the assistants went up to Donny and showed him a piece of paper. Gary saw his father nod.

Gary skated to the bench, and Coach Mulligan waved him over. "You're on Murphy's line, okay? Or does your father have an opinion on that as well?" The Coach took a chomp out of his cigar and spat it out under the bench.

"Just ignore him," Todd whispered, as he jumped out onto the ice to start the game. "Have a good game." Todd winked and Gary managed a weak smile in return.

He looked up in the stands again, hoping to see Dmitri. The young Russian had promised to come to the game. Usually that would have made Gary nervous. But the whole incident with Coach Mulligan had left him feeling kind of queasy and Dmitri's presence would just make it worse. Thankfully, there was still no sign of Rushkov. Gary didn't play much in the first period. In the second period, he could feel himself starting to fade. By the third period, he'd been sitting so long he was starting to feel chilled.

The Abbies were struggling, down 4–2 midway through the third. Gary sat on the bench, silently willing the Coach to move him up to the second line, or better yet, the first. But Coach Mulligan kept passing over Gary as he juggled the lineup, trying to generate some goals. Finally, Gary slid over next to Todd.

"Why won't he put me on?" Gary hissed.

Todd shrugged. "Nothing's going to help today."

The final score was 5–2 for O'Leary, a team the Abbies almost always beat. Coach Mulligan stormed into the dressing room after the game. He threw his clipboard down on his desk. One of the players quickly turned off the music. There was a moment of ominous silence.

"That was one of the most pathetic displays I have ever seen," the Coach fumed. "Yes, we had a little disruption before the game began..." Gary squirmed uncomfortably as his teammates looked over in his direction. "But the rest of you have no excuse. Your heads are not scrambled. So, don't play like they are. MacDonald, get back in shape. I obviously need some offence and we're not going to get it until you're back up to speed."

Gary felt a surge of pleasure as he packed up his gear. He was still on the Abbies and, even better, the Coach appeared to be promising to move him up again. He vowed he would work harder than ever to get back into shape.

Gary's smile faded when he walked into the hallway and saw the expression on his father's face. They walked to the minivan in silence. His father started the engine and then turned it off again. "I don't *ever* want to hear you say that you're quitting," his father said in a quiet but stern voice. "We are not a family of quitters. If you have a problem, work it out. But you don't quit."

Donny's voice grew louder as he continued to speak. "Of course, your mother isn't necessarily a good example. She decided to quit. But that's her choice. My children do not give up on anything. And another thing. Your attitude toward Lisa was embarrassing to me and unfair to her. It's not her fault that your mother left. It's not her fault that you had a concussion. So, from now on, I'd like you to treat her with some respect. Am I clear?"

Gary nodded. Donny turned the engine on again, just as Gunner came up and tapped on Gary's window. He quickly rolled it down.

"Dmitri wanted me to tell you," the old trainer gasped, trying to catch his breath. "He's been called up. He's sorry he missed your game."

Before Gary could say anything, Gunner had disappeared, hobbling back into the arena.

DMITRI'S DEBUT 13

GARY SAT AWKWARDLY on the new leather couch in his mother's living room. A tiny Christmas tree was lit up in one corner of the room, and behind it, through the window, the lights of the other shoreline could be seen across the harbour.

Gary had reluctantly agreed to spend the weekend at his mother's place while his father and Lisa went shopping in Halifax. Gary had a game that weekend in North River, so he couldn't go along—though he wasn't sure he would have been invited anyway.

"Isn't this a cool apartment?" Maggie whispered. Gary nodded in a noncommittal way. He still wasn't totally comfortable with his mother's new lifestyle, but he noticed that she'd worked hard to make him feel at home. Hockey posters hung in the spare room and all his favourite foods filled the refrigerator.

"What time is your game tomorrow?" his mother asked, carrying in their supper. Gary was surprised that she wasn't making them sit and eat at the table. His mother used to be very strict about suppertime. He noticed that her hair looked different, too. His mother caught him looking at her.

"Oh, you finally noticed," she laughed. "I had Paula take the grey out. Do you like it?"

"It's great, Mom," Maggie piped in. Gary just nodded.

As he ate his potatoes and meatloaf, he wondered why his parents were both, all of a sudden, so worried about looking young. His father was going to the gym every day now, and had asked Gary to come shopping with him one evening. He'd bought a leather jacket and a pair of matching boots. They weren't the kind of clothes he'd ever worn before. And now his mom was dying her hair.

"How's the training going?" she asked. "I made meatloaf because I thought it was a good way to get some weight on you. There's lots more if you want another helping."

"He's constantly on the exercise bike," Maggie explained. "If he worked that hard at school, he'd be a genius."

"Well, at least, I *could* be a genius," Gary ribbed his sister.

"You got an exercise bike?"

"Yeah, Dad gave it to me for my birthday. It's great. I don't have to go to the gym. I have my own set of weights, too. I mean, we have so much room now..." Gary stopped himself suddenly.

"Now that I've taken all the furniture. Yes, I know," his mother chided. "I'm sure your dad will eventually want to get some things that are more to his taste." Gary squirmed in his chair. He still didn't want to admit that his mother was never coming back.

"Which reminds me. Did you like my present?" his mom asked, changing the subject. Gary nodded guiltily. Last weekend, on his birthday, he had said he was too busy with hockey to see his mom. She had dropped off a package anyway.

Much to his delight, she'd given him a Snow Dogs jersey—with his name and number on the back.

"Yeah, it's cool," he mumbled, reluctant to give his mother too much credit.

"Are you going to ask him?" Maggie asked her mom.

Martha shot a stern look at her daughter. Gary glanced up from his meatloaf to see his mother staring at him.

"I, uh, was wondering if you'd mind if I brought a friend to your game tomorrow. His name is Darrell. He's my, uh, friend," his mother was almost blushing as she pushed her food around on her plate, not even looking at Gary.

"Do you have to?" Gary snapped. "It's not as if things are going so great right now. The last thing I need is more pressure."

"Well, in fact, he's on his way over now to watch tonight's game on television," his mother snapped back. "So, I guess we can skip your game tomorrow."

"Thanks for giving me so much notice," Gary shouted at his mother, pushing his plate away. "And I don't need to put on weight. So you can keep your stupid meatloaf!"

He instantly regretted his words, but he was too mad to apologize. Martha got up from the couch and ran into the kitchen.

"Way to go," Maggie whispered. "It's taken her weeks to tell you about Darrell because you've been such a baby about this whole thing."

"I'm not being a baby. I just want my family back the way it was," Gary hissed back.

"Well, that's not going to happen," his sister replied gently. "I'm just tired of everyone fighting. Couldn't you just let her have her way so that we don't have to fight about it?"

"That's not fair. Why don't *we* ever get to have a say in all of this?" Gary lowered his voice even further. "And who is Darrell, anyway?"

"I'll tell you later," Maggie whispered. "But he's nice."

"I'm sorry, Gary," Martha said, bringing a chocolate cake in from the kitchen and sliding it onto the coffee table in front of her son. "I know this has been tough on you. If you don't want Darrell to come over—"

"Hey, look!" Gary interrupted. He pointed to the television where Bobby Dawson and Russ Scott were introducing *Hockey Night in Canada.*

"Take a look at this," Bobby Dawson was saying. Gary gasped as Dmitri appeared on the screen. Suddenly, an Albany River Rats player came up and hooked him. Dmitri took a swing and then the benches emptied, led by Duffy.

"It's the fight from a couple of weeks ago," Gary explained to his mother and sister. "That's how Dmitri got all the stitches."

"Now here's the real hero," Dawson continued. "This Duffy guy sticks his neck out to save the Russky, and he gets suspended by the league for his trouble. And then the Snow Dogs trade him. Just for being a stand-up guy. That's what's wrong with Canadian hockey today. And look, the sucky Russian has to wear his visor all the time now. Waaah! Waaah!"

Gary was speechless. Bobby Dawson was making fun of Dmitri! It was so unfair.

"So you think the Islanders are going to be looking for Rushkov tonight?" Russ Scott asked.

"Oh, yeah. The Russian's going to get quite the introduction to the NHL. You can count on it," Dawson replied. "You see, Duffy's brother plays for the Islanders. I think it's going to be payback time."

"Oh no," Gary muttered. His mother looked at her son for an explanation. "He's not a suck, Mom. He's a great player. But they pick on him because he's from Russia," Gary told her, looking at Maggie for help.

"And Duffy is the one who got that girl pregnant. That's why he got traded. Everyone knows that," his sister continued.

"Obviously, someone forgot to tell Bobby Dawson," their mother replied grimly. The phone rang and Martha answered it.

"Gary, it's Todd," his mom said. Gary looked surprised, then remembered that he had told his friend to pick him up at his mom's place tomorrow for the game.

"Did you see it?" Todd said eagerly.

"Yeah. Poor Dmitri," Gary replied.

"They're all going to pick on him now."

"Do you think he'll be alright?"

"Oh yeah, the Snow Dogs have their tough guys ready to protect him."

Gary hoped his friend was right. As he settled in to watch the game, he realized that he and his mom had never finished their conversation about Darrell. Suddenly, the buzzer rang.

"Oh, it's Darrell. I, uh, didn't get a chance to call him," Martha said apologetically. "I'll just run down to the lobby and explain."

"Mom!" Gary waved his mother down as she headed to the door. "Don't worry about it. It's okay." Maggie gave him a reassuring smile and his mother looked grateful.

The door opened and Gary caught his breath. Mr. Doucette stood in his mother's front hallway. His English teacher. Could this get any worse?

"Hey Gary, how are you doing?" his teacher asked. He gave Gary's mom a peck on the cheek. "Just in time for the game, eh?"

"Bobby Dawson just did a big takeout on Dmitri, calling him a wimp and stuff," Maggie explained.

"He's the player you and Gary know, right?" Darrell said brightly, hanging up his jacket. Martha passed him a beer and he settled into the armchair.

Gary was surprised that Mr. Doucette knew about Dmitri, but he was still too shocked to say anything. How could his mother not have told him she was dating his teacher? He could just imagine what Justin and the others were going to say when they found out. Just then, Dmitri hopped over the boards for his first shift.

"Go, Dmitri," Maggie cheered. Gary held his breath. He watched his friend zigzag up and down the ice. He noticed that the Islanders were changing their shifts. He strained to see who they were putting on.

"He's such a good skater. He'll be fine," Darrell said in a reassuring voice. "That Bobby Dawson is just a blowhard. The Snow Dogs won't let anyone near Dmitri."

One of the Islanders skated right at Dmitri and nonchalantly hooked him with his stick.

"Hey, that's a penalty!" Maggie shouted.

"Why didn't they call it?" Gary echoed.

Darrell shrugged. "I think they're going to let them play and see what happens. Believe me, the refs know what's going on and they'll be keeping an eye on it."

Gary breathed a sigh of relief when Dmitri's first shift was finally over. He gave a cheer when the TV cameras cut to a shot of Dmitri on the bench, wiping his visor.

The Islanders were all over Dmitri every time he was on the ice. Gary could relate to his friend's frustration. The defencemen for the Islanders were much bigger and heavier than the young Russian and they clutched at him whenever he entered their zone. Gary wondered if Dmitri was worried. He knew it was important to rack up some points. If he didn't, the Snow Dogs might send him back to the farm team.

Finally, late in the third, Dmitri shook his defender loose. He made a nifty deke, and then fooled the goalie into going down early.

"Dmitri Rushkov scores!" boomed the announcer.

"A goal! His first NHL goal!" Gary shouted.

The living room erupted in cheers. Gary noticed that even his mom was celebrating, though he squirmed when he saw Mr. Doucette put his arm around his mother's waist. At the same time, he was surprised at how comfortable he was watching the game with his teacher. He had always liked Mr. Doucette. He just wished it wasn't *his* mother that the teacher was dating.

"I wonder if Tatiana is watching back in Russia?" Maggie asked. "That would be so romantic."

"Who's Tatiana?" her mother asked. Maggie explained.

"Maybe Dmitri will be able to bring her over sooner rather than later," Darrell Doucette suggested. "This kid is good. I think he'll be staying in New Mexico."

Gary felt a mix of emotions. Of course he was happy for his friend, but at the same time, he was going to miss Dmitri. Who was going to help him get back in shape now? Gary watched the rest of the game in silence, thinking about his friend and wondering if he would ever see him again.

BUSTED **14**

OVER THE NEXT couple of days, the Island papers were filled with news of Dmitri Rushkov's success in the NHL. It was almost as if he was an honourary Islander and the locals were anxious to claim some role in his success.

"Bobby Dawson was wrong again," one commentator pointed out.

"That's what happens when Dawson decides to put down a Russian," another added. "The kid turns into one of the best rookie prospects this season."

Unfortunately, Dmitri's big-league success was hurting the Snow Dogs. Attendance at the last game before the Christmas break had been down to around twelve hundred people. The team even had a Santa Claus in the stands handing out gifts, and Darby Sanders had been doing a ticket promotion all week at the local mall.

"It's Christmas. Everyone's busy," his father suggested. "I'm sure it will perk up in the new year."

"I'm hearing rumblings that the team is threatening to pull out," Lisa replied.

It was Christmas Eve and Lisa had spent the evening helping Gary and his dad put up the Christmas tree and decorations around the house. It was strange watching some-one else handle the same decorations that his mother and father had put up for years, but Gary was trying hard not to start a fight. Now that both his mother and father were dat-ing other people, Gary was finding it harder and harder to imagine his parents together again.

"How can they pull out?" Donny questioned. "They just got here."

Lisa shrugged. "A friend of mine is friends with Cheryl Porter. She's been told that the team will decide some time in January if they're going to stay. Apparently there's a rink being built somewhere in the States that's shopping around for a franchise."

"Are they even allowed to do that, Dad?" Gary asked.

"I'd say it's bad PR, but yeah, I guess they can. It's a busi-ness, after all."

The phone rang just then, and Gary raced to answer it. He and Todd had to work out who would drive them to their Boxing Day tournament.

"You're not going to believe this," Todd gasped. "Guess what happened to Justin?"

What had Justin done this time?

"He's in the hospital. You know those pills he gave you? Well, they made him sick, too! He started throwing up in the middle of the mall and they had to rush him to Emergency."

"Is he going to be okay?"

"Yeah," Todd replied. "But he's in a ton of trouble. And it gets worse. He's blaming you. He said you gave him the pills."

Gary could hardly believe what Todd was saying. "He can't do that!"

"Bartlett and all his buddies are covering for him. They told Coach Mulligan that you had the pills in the dressing room."

"He's never going to believe them over me!" Gary insisted.

A beep interrupted their conversation. "There's someone on the other line. I'll call you right back."

Gary clicked the receiver and said hello. It was Coach Mulligan's voice. "Hello, Gary. I need to talk to your dad."

"But Coach, I didn't do it! I had nothing to do with it..."

"Gary, let me talk to your dad."

Gary called his father. He held his hand over the mouthpiece as he filled his dad in on what had happened.

"Justin Johnston got sick from those horse pills. Now he's saying that I gave them to him! You know I didn't. Dr. Champion told me to warn him, but I was too scared. Coach Mulligan wants to talk to you."

Donny took the phone. "Vince, what's going on?"

Gary watched anxiously as his father listened to what the Coach had to say. Finally, his father spoke. "I don't totally agree with how you're handling this, but yes, I agree the boys need to be sent a message. I'll pass the information on to Gary. Yes, we'll talk to you in the new year." Donny hung up the phone.

"What do you mean the new year? We have a tournament starting the day after tomorrow," Gary said anxiously.

His father sighed. "The team has to do a full investigation. Coach Mulligan doesn't think you had anything to do with it, but Justin's dad is insisting that they check it out. And since they can't do anything until after New Year's, you're suspended until they get some answers."

"What? If he knows I didn't do anything…" Gary cried.

Donny waved his hands in the air, signalling Gary to calm down. "Whoa, Gary. This is a serious charge. And the fact of the matter is that some of the other players say that they saw you with the pills. And I know you took at least one. This is dangerous stuff. All of you need to understand just how dangerous it is."

"But I didn't do anything wrong!"

"Yes, you did! You took an illegal substance. And even worse, you took it when you didn't even know what it was. You could have ended up in Emergency just like Justin. You boys need to learn that you can't mess around with this stuff. It's wrong."

"I know it's wrong. I told you that."

"Well, now you'll have to tell Coach Mulligan, and whoever else is doing this investigation as well. There's nothing I can do, Gary. Let's just forget it until after Christmas."

The phone rang again. Gary ran from the room and headed up the stairs. He stopped near the top of the stairs, curious to hear what his father was going to say.

"Sorry, Todd, Gary won't be able to play in the tournament. That's all I can say. Good night… and Merry Christmas." Donny hung up the phone.

"Oh yeah, some Christmas this is!" Gary slammed his door and threw himself on his bed. Downstairs he could hear his father's voice as he explained to Lisa what had happened.

ABOUT AN HOUR LATER, Gary heard the front door open and close. He made his way downstairs and peered out the window and saw Lisa and his father getting into her car. He remembered his dad saying that they had a few last-minute errands to run.

Maggie was already over at their mom's, and he was supposed to be joining her there. They had all agreed that he and Maggie would spend Christmas Eve with their mother and Christmas Day at their dad's.

Right now, though, Gary wasn't in the mood for anything to do with Christmas. Reluctantly, he picked up the phone— if he was going, Maggie would have to come pick him up. But then he changed his mind. He pulled on his boots and jacket and headed out the door. At first, he wasn't sure where to go. Out of habit, he turned toward the Civic Centre. He would call Maggie once he got there. But first, he needed some time to think.

The arena was dark and the parking lot empty when Gary finally trudged the last block through the snow. The box office had closed early, and the players had long since finished their practice. The team was heading out on a road trip on Boxing Day and Gary noticed that the bus was already parked alongside the arena. He decided to try the back door. There were drifts of snow all along the side of the rink and Gary shivered slightly as the gusts of wind hit him. The walk over had warmed him up, but now he realized just how cold it was. What if the arena was locked? Where was he going to go? He wasn't even sure what time it was.

Gary's heart sank when he saw that the door was closed shut. Now what? He pulled on the handle in frustration, rattling the door in its steel frame. He gave it a final kick, and turned to go. Suddenly, the door swung open.

"Whaddya want, kid?" It was Socky Mulligan, Coach's brother. Gary had never really talked to Socky before, but he'd watched him for years, driving the Zamboni and cleaning up around the rink. He remembered, too, the story about Socky's broken foot and his lost NHL career.

"I, uh, I'm looking for Gunner," Gary stammered.

"They're all gone. Been gone for hours," Socky barked back. A strong smell of alcohol wafted over from the old man.

"Could I just come in and use the phone?" Gary pleaded. "I...play for the Abbies. I mean, I did."

"Stop your blubbering and come in out of the cold," Socky said and swung the door open. Gary just barely managed to grab it. He followed the old man into the darkness.

As his eyes adjusted to the lack of light, Gary heard voices coming from the rink, a radio broadcast of some sort. It sounded rough and scratchy, like something from one of those old shows on the History Channel. He strained to see inside the arena as Socky fumbled with the lock on the dressing room. Socky finally pulled open the door, and the light from the room shone on the old man. Gary was surprised to see him wearing an old Boston Bruins jersey. He was even more shocked when he noticed a pair of old-fashioned skates on Socky's feet.

Gary wanted to ask what was going on, but something about the look on Socky's face made him reconsider. "Here's the phone, boy," Socky said.

Gary nervously dialled his mother's number. It was busy.

Reluctantly, he turned to face Socky. "It's busy," he said apologetically. "I'll have to try again in a few minutes."

"Yeah, fine," slurred the old man. He turned awkwardly on

his skates and headed back toward the arena. "Just pull the door shut when yer done."

Gary heard him shuffle off down the corridor. He tried his mom's number again. Still busy. Coming to the arena had been a big mistake. He was beginning to picture himself trapped there for hours—just him and old Socky Mulligan. What else could go wrong? And what was the old hockey player up to?

15 SOCKY'S SECRET

GARY WAS GETTING frustrated now. His mother's line was still busy. It was probably Maggie, gabbing to one of her friends, and Gary knew from experience that that could go on for a very long time. He looked around the dressing room. Each cubicle had a name tag and player's number above it. He felt a pang of sadness as he saw Dmitri's bunk sitting empty. Usually, Gary would have been thrilled to be in the Snow Dogs' locker room, but tonight, he was more anxious to get home. Still, he was curious about Socky Mulligan. Gary spotted an old skate tossed in a corner. He used it to prop open the locker room door, and he quietly made his way down the corridor toward the arena.

As he got closer, the strange radio voices grew louder. Occasionally, they were accompanied by cheering. It was an old hockey game! An old radio broadcast of some long-forgotten match. But where was it was coming from? Gary followed the sound down the corridor leading to the penalty box area. The door was open, but the arena was dark. Suddenly, a figure skated by in the darkness. It was Socky Mulligan! Gary stood, frozen with fascination. Every couple of seconds the old man swept by the open doorway. Carefully, Gary made his way to the boards.

"And Mulligan carries the puck down the ice..." The broadcaster was talking about Socky! "He shoots, he scores!"

Down the ice, Gary saw the old man shoot the puck at the net. He raised his arms in victory as the puck slid into the empty net. Gary realized that Socky was on his way back to the bench. He ran quickly back up the corridor to get out of the old man's view. Back in the safety of the main passageway, he waited for the figure to go past again.

The minutes seemed to drag by. Where had Socky gone? Gary was about to turn and head back to the locker room to call his mother, but he decided to take one last look, just to see what the old man was up to now. He carefully edged along the corridor to the open doorway. No sign of the old hockey player. Gary leaned out the doorway and looked down the ice. Nothing. He crossed over to the other side, where he had last seen the hockey player celebrating his goal.

Gary gasped as he saw a figure slumped on the ice. He jumped over the boards. Gary moved as quickly as he could across the ice. "Are you okay?" Finally, he slid down beside the prone figure. The old man's eyes were open. Gary gagged slightly from the powerful scent of alcohol emanating from Socky's mouth. The radio broadcast was over now, and Mulligan's raspy breaths were the only sound.

"Help," the old man gasped. "Get help."

"I can't just leave you here on the ice," Gary replied. "Can you get up?"

The old man shook his head. "Help."

"Okay. I'll go phone. I'll be right back."

Gary slid quickly across the ice and then sprinted down the hallway. He was shaking so hard that he almost lost his grip on the door to the locker room when he pulled out the skate. He nervously dialled 9-1-1. "I'm at the Civic Centre. Socky Mulligan's hurt. Please help him," Gary gasped through the telephone.

"We'll be right there. What's your name?" the operator asked.

"Gary MacDonald. Socky's lying on the ice."

"Okay, Gary, calm down. How can the ambulance crew get in?"

"The back door. I'll go and open it now."

"Gary, the ambulance will be there in a few minutes. Meet them at the back door. And son... you did a good job."

Gary raced to the back door and stood shivering in the wind and snow. Finally, he heard the sirens. The ambulance pulled up and the attendants leaped out, grabbing a stretcher from the back of the van.

"Where is he, kid?" they asked. "Show us the way."

"Aren't there any lights in here?" they muttered as they followed Gary along the hallway.

"It's Christmas Eve. He's the only one here," Gary explained.

The attendants gave Gary a strange look when they got to the open door. He watched as they made their way across the ice and bent to begin working on Socky.

"What's going on? Why is there an ambulance here?" Gary turned to face Coach Mulligan.

"Over there. Socky. He just... collapsed." Gary sputtered.

Coach Mulligan walked gingerly across the ice and joined the attendants. They were gently lifting the old man onto the stretcher and strapping him in. Then the group made their way carefully off the ice.

Gary wanted to ask them if Socky was going to be okay. The old man's face was a pasty white colour and he was still breathing heavily, though the oxygen mask on his face seemed to help a bit. Gary thought he saw Socky nod at him as the attendants lifted him past.

"I'll be right behind you," Coach Mulligan told the crew, who continued down the hallway.

The Coach turned to Gary. "What are you doing here on Christmas Eve? And what happened?"

"I, uh, I was just walking around and I needed to use the phone. I don't know what Socky was doing." Gary wasn't sure how much to tell his coach.

Coach Mulligan sighed. He pointed to the tape deck. "This is Socky's annual Christmas ritual. He listens to himself on the radio, scoring his only goal in the bigs. And he shares a drink or two with the hockey gods."

"He was out there skating and then, I think, he fell," Gary said softly.

"He's too old for such foolishness," the Coach replied. "The fellows say he bumped his head. I was just on my way over to check on him when I saw the ambulance. He's going to be fine. That's the important thing."

Gary gave a sigh of relief. Then he caught a glimpse of the clock on the wall. "It's almost nine o'clock!"

"Is there somewhere you're supposed to be?" Coach Mulligan demanded, though not as sternly as usual.

"I was supposed to be at my mom's...uh...a couple of hours ago," Gary confessed.

"I'll take you there on my way to the hospital," the Coach replied. "I'll call your mother from the locker room and tell her where you are. Just help me clean up all this stuff first."

The two worked in silence. Gary noticed that a smile danced across Mulligan's face as he collected up the old Boston Bruins memorabilia that his brother had scattered across the bench.

NEITHER OF THEM SPOKE until they were in the Coach's truck heading toward Gary's mother's apartment.

"I'd appreciate if you didn't mention this to anyone," Coach Mulligan said, somewhat sheepishly. "Socky's a good fella and works hard. He just hasn't had too many breaks in life."

Gary nodded. He wanted to ask the Coach more about Socky's story but decided he probably knew all he needed to know.

"And MacDonald. Don't worry about this thing with Johnston. I'll take care of it. Just take it easy over the holidays, keep working out, and you'll be back in the lineup when the regular schedule begins. Okay?"

Gary tried not to look surprised. "Thanks, Coach."

"Just stay away from those pills. I can't believe any of my boys would be into stuff like that."

The truck pulled up in front of Gary's mother's apartment building. Gary noticed his father's car parked a little ways down the street. He waved goodbye to the Coach and pressed the buzzer. His mother's anxious voice came over the intercom.

"Oh, Gary. Are you alright? We've been so worried!"

"Mom, I'm fine."

As Gary made his way down the hallway toward his mother's apartment, the door swung open. His mother grabbed him and gave him a big hug.

"Gary! Coach Mulligan called us from the rink. What happened?" she asked, her face tense with concern.

"I went for a walk. I was going to call you from the Civic Centre. Socky Mulligan was there. He was skating, and he fell and hit his head," Gary explained. He was trying to avoid any questions about why he was at the rink in the first place.

"Is Socky going to be okay?" his father asked.

"How did he hit his head?" Lisa asked.

Gary was momentarily taken aback. He looked over at the couch and was surprised to see Lisa sitting there with Darrell. Maggie gave him an amused smile.

"What were you doing at the Civic Centre, Gary? When we left, you were supposed to call Maggie to come and pick you up," Donny MacDonald questioned his son.

"We can sort that out later," Martha suggested. "Come have something to eat."

"No, we'll sort it out now," Donny insisted. "We can't have him running all over Charlottetown in the middle of a snowstorm. What's going on?"

"Dad, I don't want to talk about it now. Everything's okay with the Coach. And Socky's going to be okay, too," Gary tried to smooth the waters. His father didn't look happy but he went into the living room to sit with Lisa.

"Dad says you're suspended," Maggie piped in.

"Maggie, I think we could all use a break right now," Darrell said nervously, watching the colour drain from Martha's face.

"I don't think we need to air our dirty laundry in public," Donny agreed.

"This isn't exactly public, Dad. This is family," Maggie persisted.

"Not exactly," her father corrected her. "Martha, we should let you enjoy the rest of your Christmas Eve with the kids and...uh...Darrell. We'll see you tomorrow, Maggs, Gary. Good night."

Donny went to the closet and took out his coat and Lisa's.

"Merry Christmas," Lisa said as they stood awkwardly at the door. "Thanks, Martha. It was nice to meet you, Darrell."

"Good night," Donny added. "Merry Christmas all. Martha..." He turned abruptly and headed out the door.

"Well, that was fun," Maggie said after a few seconds of silence.

"It wasn't a problem, Maggie," her mother chided. "They were just worried. And it made sense for them to come over here so we could all figure out together where Gary was."

"They're both very nice," Darrell added.

"Maybe you can—" Maggie stopped as she noticed the expression on her mother's face.

"Gary, are you sure you're okay?" asked his mother.

"Yeah, Mom. It's just kind of a weird Christmas," Gary replied. He felt a wave of sadness as he recalled the ghostly vision of Socky Mulligan, trying to recapture the magic of his former hockey glory. It reminded him, in some ways, of the old black-and-white Christmas movies that his mom liked to watch at this time of year. In the movies, though, there was always a happy ending. Gary wasn't sure that Socky's story had one, or ever would.

"Let's open our presents!" Maggie shouted, pulling Gary back to reality.

"Yeah, let's open our presents," Gary echoed. The old hockey player was soon forgotten amid a flurry of wrapping paper, ribbons, and laughter.

16 BIG-LEAGUE TROUBLE

COACH MULLIGAN WAS TRUE to his promise. Gary still sat out the Boxing Day tournament, but he was back on the team in January. Todd reported that the Coach had lectured the entire team on the dangers of taking any kind of steroids. He had also demanded the truth about where Justin had gotten the steroids. Threatened with a permanent suspension from the team, two of Justin's friends reluctantly admitted that they were lying about Gary's involvement. They got off easy with a three-game suspension. Justin, meanwhile, was kicked off the team for the rest of the season.

"And Coach says if anyone else is caught using steroids, he'll turn them in to the police," Todd told Gary, as they skated around the backyard rink. It was the last day of Christmas holidays, and the Abbies had a game on Tuesday against Summerside, now the second-place team in the league. Gary hoped he was going to be ready.

"Can he do that—turn us in to the police?" Gary asked, taking a shot on goal.

"Sure, why not?" Todd replied. "Hey, did you catch *Sportsdesk* this morning? Dmitri's playing just awesome.

He's closing in on the rookie scoring lead, and he didn't even get called up until December."

"Yeah, he's doing great, but I miss him," Gary replied. "He never did get to see me play."

"See *us* play!" Todd teased and shot the puck playfully in Gary's direction.

"Hey, watch the head! I've got enough problems," Gary joked.

"It doesn't bug you anymore, does it?" Todd asked. Gary knew his friend's concern was real. The boys had talked a lot this winter about how tough it was to be injured and out of hockey. Every once in a while, Todd admitted that his arm still wasn't as strong as it had been before the hit. Gary felt guilty every time the topic came up, but he knew Todd wasn't trying to make him feel that way. He and Todd were best friends—no matter what.

Gary shrugged. "I try not to think about it. But every time I get the slightest twinge in my head, I'm scared that it's coming back. But right now, I'm more worried about not making it back on the first line. I need to catch up to some Todd Manning guy, top scorer in the league."

"Oh, you'll never catch him!" Todd replied. And the two friends laughed, their breath creating great gusts of ice fog as they skated and glided around the rink.

LATER THAT NIGHT, Gary was getting his backpack ready for school the next day when the phone rang.

"Gary," a voice said. "It is Dmitri Rushkov."

Gary's heart jumped. It had been several weeks since Dmitri had left and his voice sounded strange, but familiar.

"Dmitri! What's up?"

"What do you mean, 'what is up'?"

"I mean, how are you?" Gary laughed.

"Not so good. I have problem and I need your help."

Gary was worried. How could *he* help Dmitri?

"I have agent. He says I must come to Charlottetown and no play until he get me better deal. I have no apartment now. Can I stay with you?"

What was Dmitri talking about?

"An agent? Dmitri, why would you *not* play? You're doing so well right now!"

"My agent, he say I not making same money like other rookies. He say I must make better deal. He try make deal for Pavel, too."

Gary didn't know what to say. He struggled to take in all of this new information while trying to spit out some sort of answer to Dmitri's question.

"Sure, you can stay with us. I mean, I have to ask my dad, but I'm sure it will be okay. When do you get here?"

"I am here now. I am at airport. But Gary, no one knows. You must keep big secret where I am."

"Okay, Dmitri. Come on over. I'll call my dad right now."

Dmitri hung up the phone. Gary stopped for a moment, trying to figure out what was going on. One thing was certain—he needed his dad. And his dad was at Lisa's. He went over to the fridge and found the piece of paper with her phone number on it.

"Gary!" Lisa sounded surprised. "How are you doing? Are you all ready for school?"

"I'm great, Lisa, thanks. Um…can I talk to my dad?"

"Gary, what's wrong?" His dad sounded worried.

"Something's happening with Dmitri. He's at the airport. His agent told him not to play. And he wants to stay with us. Can you come home?"

"I'll be right there. Just sit tight."

Gary hung up the phone and stared around the kitchen. What was going on? The phone rang again just as Donny and Lisa pulled into the driveway.

"Gary, it is Dmitri again. I must not take taxi or people will know I am here. Can you come and pick me up at airport?"

"My dad and Lisa just pulled in. We'll be right there."

On the way to the airport, Gary repeated his conversation with Dmitri to his dad and Lisa.

"Can Dmitri do this?" Lisa asked Donny.

"I'd have to know more about his contract," he replied. "I know that there are one-way and two-way contracts. One kind of contract grants players the right to be paid NHL salaries if they're called up. With the other kind, they make what they would have made playing for the farm team, with only a slight bonus if they do play in the NHL. Hopefully, Dmitri can explain what's going on."

A figure bundled up in a large coat and hat stood outside the arrival terminal, a duffel bag at his feet. Gary noticed that Dmitri didn't have his equipment with him.

"What are you doing waiting outside?" Lisa asked, opening the back door for a shivering Dmitri.

"I am worried someone will see me and phone the team," Dmitri explained.

"They don't know where you are?" Donny asked.

"It is, how you say, long story," Dmitri explained. He

smiled at Gary. "I am so happy to see you, my friend. Now I get to see you play hockey."

"But Dmitri, what about the NHL?" Gary asked. As worried as he was about Dmitri's situation, he was secretly pleased that the player remembered his promise to come and watch Gary play.

"I have new agent. He is from Russia. He say I sign bad deal. Snow Dogs try to, how you say, rip me. Now I must get better deal so I make money in NHL."

Gary was surprised to hear Dmitri talking about money. A couple of months ago, the young hockey player had been more than happy just to be in North America, making enough money to send back to Russia. Now, all of a sudden, he sounded very different.

"Where is your agent now?" Donny asked as he pulled into the driveway. Gary noticed that Dmitri looked around to see if any of the neighbours were watching.

"He is in New Mexico, talking to team. But he said I must not talk to team here. I come here because I have no place else to go. It was here or Russia, and Russia is too far." A cloud crossed over Dmitri's face.

LATER ON, Gary went to the guest room to see how Dmitri was doing. The young Russian came to the door carrying some framed photos.

"This room is very good," Dmitri smiled. "And now I take out my pictures. They go everywhere with me."

Gary noticed there were several of Dmitri and Tatiana. And another with Dmitri and an older woman.

"This is Pavel," Dmitri said, passing Gary one of the

frames. A younger version of Dmitri stared out at him. "Pavel is in big trouble. He must pay much money to some very bad men. Now he needs big contract in NHL. And my agent says he can help if I do what he tell me. I must help my brother."

"I thought Pavel didn't really want to come here," Gary said, remembering the conversation from the fall.

Dmitri shrugged. "These men say I make good NHL career. Pavel must make so too. They buy him expensive truck and give him money for gambling. Pavel loses much money. Now he must do as they say. They are very dangerous."

"Can't he go to the police?" Gary persisted.

"Russia is not like North America. The police, some time, they are as bad as the criminals," Dmitri explained. "But you must not say anything about Pavel. It would be very danger-ous for him if these men know I tell others what I know."

"Can't you tell my dad?" Gary asked. "He's a lawyer. Maybe he can help."

Dmitri shook his head. "Maybe I ask for help someday. But now, I must do as my agent says."

Gary, his father, and Dmitri watched *Sportsdesk* that evening, but there was no mention of the missing Russian.

"The Snow Dogs play tomorrow night," Gary's dad said. "They'll have to say something when he doesn't show up for the game."

He turned to the young Russian. "I wish you would let me talk to your agent. Maybe I can be of some help, or give him some advice on the North American legal system."

Dmitri shook his head as he stood up. "He is very stubborn man. I must do as he says. Good night, MacDonalds." He gave

Gary an anxious look on his way to the stairs, reminding him not to reveal their earlier conversation.

"I get the feeling there's something he's not telling us," said Donny, when he heard Dmitri's door shut.

"Good night, Dad," Gary said, leaving the room before his father had a chance to ask any more questions.

THE MISSING SUPERSTAR 17

THE FIRST DAY BACK at school seemed to drag. At lunch, Gary struggled to pay attention as Todd strategized for the Tuesday night game against Summerside.

"Gary, are you listening to anything I'm saying?" he asked, between bites of his sandwich. "Don't forget we have an extra practice tonight to work out the new lines. I'm sure Mulligan's going to move you back up to the first line."

"Don't get too comfortable, MacWuss!" Justin elbowed Gary in the head as he walked by their table. "I'll be back soon enough to take my spot on the first line."

"Why can't he just leave me alone!" Gary snapped as Justin walked away, laughing to himself.

"What's he talking about?" said Todd, shaking his head. "He's gone for the rest of the season. Everyone knows that."

"Did you hear?" Callum Wilkinson, one of their teammates, slid onto the bench beside them.

"Hear what?" Gary asked.

"Justin is taking the Abbies to court. He's suing them for kicking him off the team," Callum explained breathlessly. The boys stared at him, dumbfounded.

"You've got to be kidding," Todd said. "Coach Mulligan would never stand for that."

"He has no choice," Callum continued. "Justin's dad filed the lawsuit this morning. Everyone's talking about it."

Gary's lunch lurched in his stomach. If Justin went to court, everyone would find out that Gary had also taken one of those stupid pills. He would be the laughingstock of the entire school! He could just hear the lunch-table talk now: "Did you hear? MacDonald took a horse pill!"

The afternoon passed as slowly as the morning, and by the time Gary got home to pack up his gear, a lump had formed in his stomach. He stood by the front window, waiting for Mrs. Manning and Todd to pick him up. There was no sign of Dmitri. Gary wondered where he was. He hoped nothing else had happened. He was still worrying about Dmitri twenty minutes later as Mrs. Manning turned into the Civic Centre parking lot.

"What's going on here? I wonder," she said, pulling up in front of the main entrance. There were news trucks parked all over the place and people were rushing inside.

"I don't know, but I hope Dmitri's okay," Gary muttered, grabbing his hockey bag and rushing toward the entrance.

"Dmitri?" Todd asked as he struggled to keep up with his friend.

"I'll tell you later."

The boys scurried past the crowd and made their way around the corridor to the locker room. They could hear Coach Mulligan's voice before they even opened the door.

"I will not stand for this kind of garbage. I've had enough of these shenanigans," Coach Mulligan shouted at no one in particular. "First, Manning almost has his shoulder broken by one of his teammates. Then MacDonald gets his bell rung. Now I have a bunch of kids taking horse pills *and* I'm getting sued!" The Coach took the whistle from around his neck and tossed it at Russ, the assistant coach. "They're all yours. I'm through." Mulligan stormed out of the dressing room. The players froze, watching the door slowly swing shut.

After a moment's silence, Russ grabbed the whistle and gave a blast. "Okay, that's enough. Five minutes until practice. Get a move on. We've got a big game tomorrow."

Russ gestured to the other assistant coach and they headed out the door.

"Now we're going to lose for sure," Callum said, sinking onto the bench.

"C'mon guys. Coach Mulligan will be back," Todd urged his teammates.

"Yeah, and so will Justin. And boy, oh boy, is he going to have your ass," Doug Currie, one of the older boys, teased Gary. Gary just turned his back and kept on getting dressed.

The door swung open again. "Which one of you is Gary MacDonald?" Gary turned to see the heavy frame of Clark Dinsmore blocking the doorway. The boys looked shocked to see the Snow Dogs' president in their dressing room.

"I'm Gary," Gary said in a weak voice.

"Come with me, kid."

"I don't think so." Gary heard his dad's voice from outside the door.

"Who are you?" Dinsmore snapped.

"Donny MacDonald. Gary's father, and a lawyer with the firm of Potter, Hunt, and Martin. Was there something you needed to ask my son?"

Dinsmore stepped out into the hallway, with Gary close behind. The door shut behind him with a gentle click.

Donny pulled Gary aside and spoke to him in a low voice. "I thought there might be trouble down here. Apparently, Dmitri's agent let it slip that Dmitri was here in Charlotte-town. The team put two and two together and figured out he was probably staying with us. The media found out, and I've had reporters calling me for the last couple of hours. But don't worry, Dmitri's fine. Just concentrate on practice. I'll be here the whole time." He gave Gary a confident slap on the back and turned to face off with the Snow Dogs' president. Gary returned to the dressing room.

"What is going on?" Todd asked his friend.

"I'll tell you later," Gary whispered, sensing all eyes on them. "Dmitri's here."

"Here?" Todd asked. Gary shushed him.

"Maybe you're being sued now, too," another player joked from across the room.

The joke broke the tension in the room. Everyone laughed and turned their attention back to getting dressed.

Donny MacDonald stayed in the stands for the entire prac-tice. Gary glanced up at his father several times trying to get some clue as to what was going on. He was so distracted that he almost missed the big news: he'd been moved up to the first line and reunited with Todd.

"Together again, my friend," Todd gave him a high-five as they skated off the ice.

Suddenly, a reporter with a TV cameraman in tow came racing around the corner.

"There he is," she pointed at Gary. The camera's light shone on Gary's and Todd's faces and they squinted in the bright glare.

"Where is he?" the reporter shouted. "Where is Dmitri Rushkov?" Other reporters had appeared and a circle began to form around Gary and Todd.

Gary's dad pushed his way into the crowd. "Excuse me, I'm Gary's father," he said politely but firmly. "My son won't be answering any questions. Please let these boys through."

The cameraman swung around and pointed his equipment at Donny. "Where is he? Is it true that Rushkov is in Charlottetown?"

Gary didn't hear any more of the questions. Russ appeared out of nowhere and pushed the two boys along the corridor and into the dressing room.

"You could have warned me," he snarled. "It's not as if we don't have enough problems around here, without you harbouring a missing superstar!"

"What is going on?" Todd interjected. "Gary?"

"It's Dmitri. I guess he's left the team. He's hiding out... somewhere. I can't tell you where," Gary explained dejectedly. "I didn't think everyone was going to find out so soon."

"I just want your minds on the game tomorrow night," Russ said firmly. "This is Summerside we're playing. We can't fool around. Eye on the puck, boys."

"What about Coach Mulligan?" someone asked.

"Leave that to me," Russ replied. "He'll be back. It's just a question of when."

Gary's dad appeared in the doorway. "C'mon, Gary. The cameras are gone. And we've got to get home."

"I'll call you later," Gary whispered to Todd as he grabbed his hockey gear.

AS THEY DROVE the snowy streets back to their house, Donny filled Gary in. "The Snow Dogs held a press conference in New Mexico a few hours ago. They said that Dmitri is not in the lineup because he's holding out for more money and pushing for an NHL contract for his brother," Donny explained. "The commentators are having a field day with this—according to them, Dmitri's a greedy Russian who's holding his team to ransom. They're making him look really bad."

"I don't know what to believe," he continued, shaking his head. "Dmitri finally gave me his agent's name, so I've had some of our investigators checking him. It seems this Vladimir Smolikin is not the most reliable character around. He may even have some ties to the Russian mafia. I called the English language newspaper in Moscow and they're faxing some articles about him to the office. Lisa's going to bring them over later."

"The Russian mafia!" Gary exclaimed. "You mean like the bad guys in the gangster movies?"

"Well, not exactly," said Donny. "But they are criminals and it's not good for Dmitri to be involved with them, that's for sure! Did he ever mention any of this to you?" Donny asked as he turned into their driveway.

"Uh, not the mafia," Gary paused, not wanting to betray his friend's secret. "But he did say something about his brother, Pavel."

Donny turned to his son, surprised. "What about Pavel?" He turned off the engine but motioned to Gary to stay in the car.

"I guess Pavel's in some kind of trouble. Maybe with the mafia. Dmitri didn't say. But he really needs an NHL contract, or else," Gary explained reluctantly.

"Or else what?"

"I don't know. Dmitri didn't say. But don't tell him I told you."

Donny's face was grim as he helped Gary carry his gear into the house. He looked up and down the street, as if expecting to see someone.

"Do you think they're coming here?" Gary asked, following his father's gaze.

"Not the mafia. The media. They're convinced that Dmitri is somewhere in Charlottetown. Because of the Adopt-a-Player program, they found out that he's friends with our family. We'll just have to be extra careful."

"But the mafia's not coming here, right?" Gary repeated anxiously.

"Gary, we'll be fine. And don't worry, we'll find some way to help Dmitri," his father reassured him as they walked into the house.

An ashen-faced Dmitri was sitting in the kitchen, watching the sports channel. "They say I am greedy, just playing for money! It is not true. The Snow Dogs say they will trade me if I do not play. But my agent says I must not. What should I do?"

"Whoa, Dmitri. Calm down. First, let's figure out exactly who we're dealing with. We need to know more about Vladimir Smolikin," Donny suggested.

Just then, Lisa walked through the back door, shaking snow off her feet. "I've got them," she said, waving a stack of papers in her hand. She and Donny sat at the table and quickly glanced over the pages. Dmitri and Gary watched them curiously.

"Well, we're a bit closer to finding out who we're dealing with," Donny said finally.

"What are these?" Dmitri asked.

"Articles from the *Moscow Times*, the top English language daily paper in Russia. I made a call to the news editor there and he faxed these over," Donny explained.

"It appears that Vladimir Smolikin has ties to the Russian mafia," Lisa continued. "And he has been involved in extortion cases involving other NHL players. In fact, the NHL Players' Association tried to have him kicked out of the United States, but at the last minute all the players refused to testify against him. He's a shady character, alright."

"How did he contact you?" Donny asked the young Russian.

"I guess I must tell you all," said Dmitri with a sigh. "He came to practice in New Mexico. I was very confused in new city, with new team. He offered to help me. Like Gary help me here," Dmitri turned to his friend and smiled. Then his smile faded.

"It was so help for me, having someone who speak my language. He help me find apartment and new truck and bank account. And then he offer to help Pavel," Dmitri continued.

"What about Pavel?" Donny encouraged him to go on. Dmitri shrugged. "I was surprised. He said he knows Pavel from Moscow. He says Pavel wants to come play now in United States."

"But you said Pavel *doesn't* want to come here. He wants to stay in Russia," Gary interjected.

"I phone Pavel. He sounds very strange on telephone. He say some men want him to come to NHL. They give him many nice things. New truck. Money for gambling. Now they say he must come play in NHL and give them money back." The Russian put his head in his hands and paused.

"How much money, Dmitri? Did he say?" Donny said gently.

"I not know. But they are very bad men," Dmitri replied. "I not want to put your family in danger. I can go if this now dangerous for you."

Donny shook his head. "This is North America, Dmitri, not Russia. The police can protect us. And from what I've been able to find out, the Russian mafia doesn't have much of a presence here yet. But the problem is how to help Pavel... and what to do about your contract."

"Have you signed anything for Vladimir Smolikin?" Lisa asked, jotting down some notes.

"I think I was signing papers for my apartment. But he says I signed deal to make him my agent, too," Dmitri replied.

Donny and Lisa exchanged looks. "What about your other agent? The one who negotiated your deal with the Snow Dogs?"

"It was someone with Red Army team," Dmitri told them. "In Russia, we don't have agents like here. We are property of teams. Our teams make deal with NHL teams."

"Okay, this is going to take some digging," Donny concluded. "Dmitri, are you willing to hire my firm to represent you? I mean, only if you feel comfortable."

Dmitri thought for a moment. "I am worried for Pavel. What will Vladimir Smolikin do when he hears I have told about our deal?"

"He's right, Donny," Lisa nodded. "We'll have to try to do this without Smolikin finding out. Dmitri, I know this is hard for you, but is there any way to get your family out of Russia?"

Dmitri looked surprised.

"I think she's right, Dmitri," Donny continued. "There is only so much we can do from here. The best thing is for Pavel to leave Russia."

"And my mother? She is very old. She doesn't want to come to Canada," Dmitri moaned. "And what about Tatiana? She will not be safe. Oh, this is such big trouble."

As the adults sat working out the details for their plan, Gary watched Dmitri struggling to understand what was going on. He felt badly for the young Russian. He seemed so much more troubled than the carefree player whom Gary had met at the Civic Centre just a few months ago.

Later, as Gary was going to bed, his father tapped on the door. He came in and sat down on the bed.

"Is everything going to be okay?" Gary asked.

His father nodded. "Our biggest challenge is to get Dmitri's family out of Russia as quickly as possible, without Smolikin catching wind of it. Dmitri is on the phone now. I just hope the Russian mafia isn't listening in."

"They can do that?" Gary demanded, his eyes widening.

"Oh, I don't know what they can or can't do," his father said, rubbing his forehead. "I've got to head back to the office and file a restraining order against Smolikin. Maggie's here…oh, and, of course, Dmitri. You should be fine."

"Dad," Gary said as his father started to close the door.

"Yes?"

"Thanks. And say thanks to Lisa, too."

Donny smiled at his son. "Get some sleep. Dmitri's safe with us."

18 DISTRACTIONS

THE NEXT DAY AT SCHOOL, Todd was waiting on the front steps when Donny dropped Gary off.

"Why weren't you on the bus? Why didn't you call me? And what's going on with Dmitri?" Todd peppered his friend with questions.

Gary tried to explain some of what was going on. "And so this agent convinced Dmitri not to play for the team. But he's really after Dmitri's money," Gary told Todd. He felt badly that he couldn't tell his friend the whole story. But Gary's dad had warned him not to mention the mafia.

As the boys were hanging up their jackets in their lockers, Justin came by and shoved Gary in the back. "I guess your dad's going to be busy for the next couple of days," Justin teased.

Gary stared back at the older boy. How did Justin know about Dmitri's problems? "Yeah, we'll see you in court, MacWuss," Justin taunted. "My dad's lawyer is calling for you as a witness. I hope your hotshot dad can get you out of this mess. Or maybe you can just lie again."

Justin roared with laughter and sauntered off down the hallway.

"Oh great, that's just what my dad needs," Gary sighed.

He called his dad's office at lunch.

"How's it going, Dad?" he asked nervously.

"Fine, Gary. But I'm kind of busy right now. Is there a problem?"

"Well, um, yeah. I forgot to tell you that Justin Johnston's dad filed something so that Justin wouldn't be suspended. And, uh, I guess I have to go to court," Gary mumbled.

He heard his father shuffling through some papers. "Gary, I'm going to have to get someone else to handle this. I'm up to my eyeballs trying to help Dmitri."

"Can Lisa do it?"

"I'll ask her. Don't worry. We'll talk about it tonight."

"I, uh, have a game tonight," Gary reminded his father.

"I don't know if I can make it, Gary. Can Maggie take you?"

Gary tried not to sound disappointed. After all, it was his first time back on the first line since before his concussion. But at least this time his dad had a good reason for missing the game.

"Sure, Dad."

"Gary, I'm sorry. But I'm sure you'll be fine."

All afternoon, Gary's stomach was filled with butterflies. He wasn't sure if he was nervous about the game, the Russian mafia, or having to testify in court about Justin's pills.

Gary made sure he ate as soon as he got home, but he could only swallow a few bites of toast. Dmitri sat at the kitchen table, watching him.

"This is good. I get to see you play hockey," Dmitri said.

Gary gave him an astonished look. "Dmitri, you can't come to my game! It's not safe. Everyone will see you."

Dmitri shook his head. "No, I am safe now. Your father is

making case against Vladimir Smolikin. My family is preparing to leave Russia. It will all be okay."

Maggie arrived just in time to overhear the last part of the conversation. "Your family is coming to Canada?"

Dmitri nodded. "Your father and Lisa make papers today to bring my family here to Charlottetown. Because they are in much danger, your government will let them come right away."

"But don't they have to pack and stuff?" Maggie asked.

"We have not many things. My mother, she is very sad. But I explain to her that it is best thing for Pavel. And Tatiana, she comes, too." Dmitri beamed with pleasure.

"When will they be here?" Gary asked.

"We hope this weekend," Dmitri replied. "I go back to Charlottetown Snow Dogs practice when my family is safe. And the Snow Dogs, they play here in Charlottetown this weekend, so it is good time for my family to come."

"Wow, this is all happening so fast," Gary exclaimed.

Dmitri nodded in agreement. "I am so happy to think my family will now be safe. And I miss playing hockey. I feel so bad for not playing for team."

"What about your contract?" Maggie inquired, ignoring the glare from her brother.

"I not know. But I have good deal with Snow Dogs before Vladimir Smolikin. I make enough money for good life in Canada," Dmitri replied.

"Shhh," Gary said. "Look, Dmitri. They're talking about you on TV."

"Those greedy foreign players. This is what happens when you let them come and take over Canadian hockey. And imagine the nerve of this Rushkov guy demanding a contract for his brother, too." The MacDonalds and Dmitri stared in astonishment at Bobby Dawson, who was waving his finger at the television camera.

"And a former teammate of Rushkov says the Russian player constantly complained about not making enough money," the announcer continued.

"Look, it's Rob Duffy," Gary exclaimed.

"Rushkov represents everything that is bad about Russian hockey. The Snow Dogs have gone downhill since he joined the team," Rob Duffy told the reporter.

"Turn it off," Gary shouted. Maggie quickly changed the channel.

Dmitri looked crushed. "Why they say these things about me?"

"Dmitri, don't worry about it. They're idiots. You know what a slime Rob Duffy is," Maggie told him.

"What is a 'slime'?" Dmitri asked. And they all laughed.

"We've got to get going," Maggie said to her brother, getting up from the kitchen table. Dmitri got up, too.

Maggie shook her head. "Dmitri. Really. It's not a good idea. You can come see one of his games some other time."

"No, I come today," Dmitri insisted.

"Gary, we've got to call Dad," Maggie said.

"We don't have time," Gary replied sharply. "I can't be late."

Maggie gave both of them an exasperated look. "If anything happens, this is all your fault," she threatened her brother.

Gary knew his sister was right but he felt powerless to change anything that was going on. I've got to concentrate on the game, he told himself. Whatever happens, happens.

GARY SAT TENSELY in the back seat while Maggie and Dmitri chatted. The Russian had not seen much of the Island beyond Charlottetown, and was captivated by the rolling farmland and colourful barns along the highway. When they arrived at the rink, Gary jumped out of the minivan. "I think you should wait here until game time," he pleaded with Dmitri.

"No. I come in to locker room with you now," Dmitri insisted. "Coach Mulligan, he say I am welcome any time."

Gary had just started to explain that Coach Mulligan wasn't there anymore when Todd appeared in his gear, waving to Gary. "C'mon, you're late." He looked surprised to see Dmitri, but didn't say anything.

The dressing room went silent as Gary and Dmitri walked in. Gary put down his bag and started to change. Dmitri introduced himself to Russ, who looked flustered.

"I, uh, it's nice to meet you," Russ mumbled. "Sure, we'd love to have you on the bench. I guess. I mean, sure."

Dmitri joined in the team huddle and cheered along with the players, who kept looking at the young Russian with wonder. Dmitri smiled as he lined up with Russ and the other assistant coaches and gave each player a high-five as they walked out of the locker room.

"You have good game, Gary." Dmitri winked as they made their way to the bench.

During the warm-up, Gary noticed people in the stands pointing at Dmitri on the bench and whispering to one another. A couple had cellphones pressed to their ears.

Gary lost the opening faceoff and things didn't go much better for the rest of the period. By the end of the first,

Summerside was up 2-0. In the locker room, Russ berated the players for their lack of concentration. "I told you this was going to be a big one. I need your best effort now, or we're going to lose first place in the division. And I don't want to be around when Coach Mulligan finds out that we've dropped to second."

When Russ finished addressing the team, he pulled Dmitri aside. To Gary, it looked as if the assistant coach was trying to explain something. He wanted to go over and help, but something about Dmitri's expression made him stop.

When the team came back out for the second period, a group of people was standing behind their bench, holding signs. As he got closer, Gary realized that they were chanting something as well.

"Russian go home! Russian go home! Russian go home!…" The protesters waved signs reading, "Good-bye to Greedy Players" and "Rotten Rushkov." "Poor Dmitri," Gary muttered.

"They're just a bunch of hicks," Todd replied. "It's not a big deal."

Just then, Gary noticed a camera crew heading toward the protesters. Gary skated over to the bench, where Dmitri was standing, looking confused.

"Go home, Dmitri. Get Maggie to drive you home," he urged, looking for his sister in the row of seats behind the bench. His eyes met hers, and she simply nodded in agreement. Reluctantly, the Russian began to make his way past the other players on the bench.

As he approached Maggie, standing in the aisle, keys in hand, one of the protesters leaned over and tossed her sign at him. Dmitri managed to duck, but the sign hit Maggie in the head. Russ raced over and helped the pair through the crowd.

Meanwhile, the referee called for the Abbies to line up.

"We've got to wait for our coach to get back," Todd protested.

"Forget it. You line up now, or you forfeit the game," the ref replied.

One of the other coaches motioned for Gary and Todd to line up. The linesman dropped the puck just as the ref blew his whistle.

"Too many men on the ice," he indicated, and motioned Gary over to the penalty box.

"Wait, don't we get to choose who goes to the box?" Gary argued.

"Look, kid. You may be friends with the big Russian superstar, but I'm in charge here. You're out of the game!" The ref signalled a game misconduct for Gary, who stood looking at him in disbelief.

Todd skated over and urged Gary off the ice. "Don't say anything else. He's obviously got it in for you. We're toast."

Gary walked to the dressing room and slumped against the lockers. He heard a cheer and groaned. Summerside had scored again.

Gary sat in the locker room for the rest of the period. He didn't want to run into the protesters or the camera crew. When the players came in between periods, Callum Wilkinson brushed into Gary.

"Thanks a lot, MacDonald. Anything more you and your Russian buddy want to do now that we're down 4–0? At least two of the goals are your fault," the player snapped.

Gary slammed his locker door in frustration. Russ glared over at the two young players.

"That's enough," Russ shouted. "They're pounding us. I don't need you twerps going after each other as well. This isn't Gary's fault. We're all in this together. The ref was wrong. We've got to live with it. Now get your minds back on this game."

"By the way, Coach Mulligan's in the stands," Gordie, the trainer, added. "I'm sure he's not happy with what he's seeing."

Russ shook his head. "If you want the Coach back, you better come out and show some guts in the third."

Gary sat in silence as his teammates filed out. The Abbies managed to score twice, but still lost the game 4–2.

THE MANNINGS WERE waiting outside the locker room when Gary and Todd came out. "We told Maggie we'd give you a ride home," Mrs. Manning told Gary.

"Is she okay?" he asked.

Todd's mom nodded. "Just a bump on her head. I think it scared her and Dmitri more than it hurt."

"Are those people gone?" Todd asked his dad.

Mr. Manning nodded. "Rink security tossed them out. I don't know where they came from, but they certainly weren't pleasant."

"How did they even know that Dmitri was here?" Gary inquired as the Mannings made their way out of the arena.

Todd's dad shrugged. "It's PEI. Everyone knows everything. And thanks to those TV cameras, everyone in North America's going to know where Dmitri is."

The boys were silent on the drive home. Gary was surprised to see a couple of cars parked outside his house when the Mannings pulled up to the driveway. He thanked Todd's parents for the ride and nervously made his way inside. His mom and Mr. Doucette were sitting in the living room along with a man that Gary didn't recognize. His dad and Lisa were there, too, a pile of papers stacked in front of them on the coffee table.

"Gary, this is Constable Collins from the RCMP," his dad said.

"Where's Dmitri?" Gary asked.

"Upstairs on the phone," Maggie replied as she came into the living room. A bandage was taped to her forehead and she gave her brother a sheepish grin when she realized he was staring at it. "It's just a tiny cut. But Mom insisted I put this on."

Gary's mom moved over on the couch, making room for her son to sit down.

"We have reason to believe that Vladimir Smolikin may try to contact Dmitri," Constable Collins explained. "So we need everyone to be on the alert."

"We've filed an injunction against him, legally removing him as Dmitri's agent," Donny said. "But we're worried that he's going to get a message back to his cohorts in Russia. And we can't get Dmitri's family out of the country until Thursday."

"Are we in any danger here?" Gary's mom asked, putting a protective arm around Gary's shoulder.

"We're convinced that the Russian mafia poses no danger to you or your family. It's Dmitri and his family that we're most concerned about," the Constable replied.

Dmitri entered the room. He gave Gary a quick smile. "You win the game?"

Gary shook his head. "We lost 4–2 to Summerside." He didn't bother to add that the referee had tossed him out. Dmitri had enough on his mind.

"What are your plans now?" Constable Collins asked the Russian player.

"Mr. MacDonald has told me it is best to tell the team the truth about why I had to leave," Dmitri said. "And I will return to the Snow Dogs team here in Charlottetown. The team will then not be so mad at me. Then we wait for my family to arrive." Dmitri's forehead creased with tension at the mention of his family.

"Is there any way to get them out of there sooner?" Donny asked Lisa. She shook her head. "It took a whole afternoon of begging just to get them on Thursday. The Canadian Embassy had to lean hard on their contacts in Moscow to make this happen. It's the best we can do."

"Do we have any idea where Smolikin is now?" Darrell asked.

"Your guess is as good as mine," Donny replied grimly. "Dmitri, what did Pavel have to say? Had he heard from Smolikin or his associates?"

"He would not tell me anything," Dmitri said sadly. "But he promised to keep my mother and Tatiana safe until they can leave on Thursday."

"What about the police in Moscow? Can they help? Or what about the Red Army organization?" Martha suggested.

"They are, how you say, corrupt," Dmitri answered. "I am not sure who I can trust now in Russia."

Constable Collins stood up and shook Dmitri's hand. "We'll do everything we can, son. The best thing for you to do is sit tight. I'll have someone watching the house, but in plain clothes." He nodded to everyone else. "Good night, folks."

"We'd better get going, too," Martha said as she and Darrell stood up. "Call us if there's anything we can do. And Gary, Darrell will make sure the teachers keep an eye on you around school."

Gary nodded in his mom's direction, but his eyes were on Dmitri. The expression on the young player's face made Gary wonder if there was something he still wasn't saying.

PAVEL **19**

WEDNESDAY PASSED IN a haze of classes and worrying. Gary could barely keep his mind off Dmitri, and as he made his way home from school, he was relieved to think that Pavel, Tatiana, and Dmitri's mom would soon be safe on a plane from Russia. But as soon as Gary walked in the back door, he could hear shouting. It sounded like Dmitri, but Gary couldn't make out what he was saying. Then he heard another voice. It was Clark Dinsmore, the president of the Snow Dogs. Gary cautiously opened the door to the kitchen and followed the voices into the living room.

"There was nothing else I could do," Dinsmore was saying. He turned abruptly when he saw Gary come in. "I'm going to have to ask you to leave, son. This is a private meeting."

"This is Gary's house, Mr. Dinsmore. And what happens with me okay for Gary to know," Dmitri replied. Gary could tell his friend was upset. Dmitri's accent was always thicker when he was tense, and two red spots had appeared on the Russian's cheeks.

"Please to call your father, Gary," Dmitri continued. "I need some help from my lawyer." He glared defiantly at Clark

Dinsmore. Gary left to use the phone in the kitchen. He paused as the two men resumed their argument.

"Dmitri, I can't help Pavel. The team has had enough of this bad publicity. It was all I could do to convince the owners to keep you," Dinsmore continued.

"But you say to cameras that Snow Dogs no want Pavel. That mean the Russian mafia hear too. You put my brother's life in danger." Dmitri's voice was getting louder and louder.

"Dad, you've got to come home now," Gary whispered into the phone. "It's Clark Dinsmore. He and Dmitri are fighting in the living room. Something about Pavel."

"I'll be right there. Don't let Dinsmore leave," Donny insisted as he hung up the phone.

Gary stood in the kitchen, not sure whether he should go back into the living room or not. The yelling had stopped, and now, a new sound made its way into the kitchen—the sound of someone crying.

"Dmitri, I'm sorry. I had no choice," Clark Dinsmore said softly as Gary edged closer to the door. Dmitri was slumped in an armchair, his head buried in his hands.

"My dad will be right home," Gary said, walking into the living room as if he hadn't been listening outside the door. "Mr. Dinsmore, can you stay for a few minutes? He'd like to talk to you."

"It is too late," Dmitri cried. "I fear for my brother. And it is your fault." He lunged out of the chair and grabbed at the lapel of Dinsmore's jacket. The larger man put out his arms and carefully pushed the young Russian back into his seat.

Dinsmore's cellphone rang and he quickly answered it. Gary and Dmitri watched carefully as he gave monosyllabic answers to the questions from the other end. Finally, he closed his phone.

"The team has had a call from Vladimir Smolikin. He's still in New Mexico. He wants to meet with the owners to work out a deal on Pavel's behalf. I guess he didn't hear the press conference earlier," Dinsmore shrugged.

"What else did he say? Does he know where Pavel is?" Dmitri asked.

"What do you mean?" Dinsmore asked.

"We don't know where Pavel is! Some men were following Tatiana and my mother on way to the Canadian Embassy. Pavel said he would try to make them follow him, so they could go safely. Then he would meet them later. But he never came."

Clark Dinsmore rubbed his forehead. "This is new information, Dmitri. We assumed that Pavel was safely on his way to Canada. We never would have mentioned him if we had thought he was in any danger."

"What's going on here?" Donny MacDonald appeared in the doorway.

"We've got a major problem," Dinsmore replied. "Pavel is missing. We announced today that we were not interested in signing him. The owners insisted that we say that for the record. At the time, we had no idea that he was missing."

"Missing?" Donny turned to Dmitri. "Since when?"

"Since few hours ago. My mother and Tatiana go to Canadian Embassy, like you say. But Pavel worry that someone follow them. He take other car. Now he not arrive at Embassy."

"But their plane leaves in a few hours!" Donny exclaimed.

He grabbed for the phone. "I've got to get our people in Moscow working on this. Damn!"

"I'm sorry, Dmitri," Clark Dinsmore said, picking up his coat. "I didn't know. All I can do now is to try to convince Smolikin that we've changed our minds about Pavel."

"This Vladimir is bad man," Dmitri replied. "He will not be easily fooled."

"I'll do what I can, Dmitri," promised Dinsmore. "In the meantime, just sit tight."

FOR THE REST of the evening, Dmitri and the MacDonalds sat anxiously by the phone waiting for word from Moscow. Around midnight, there was a call from the airport.

"Your mother and Tatiana are safely on their way to Canada," Donny said as he continued to listen. Dmitri closed his eyes for a moment and gave a heavy sigh. Donny listened again.

"There's still no sign of Pavel. He missed the flight. The Canadian Embassy has a couple of leads, though, and they hope to have more in the morning."

"That's great that your mom and Tatiana are safe," Maggie said enthusiastically, sensing Dmitri's disappointment.

The phone rang again. This time, the Canadian Embassy was on the other end. A strange expression came over Donny's face as he listened intently to the caller.

"How bad is it? Uh-huh. Tomorrow morning. Okay, fine. I'll tell him. Thank you for letting us know." Donny hung up the phone. For a moment he couldn't speak.

"What is it?" Dmitri cried.

"An anonymous caller telephoned the Embassy. He said Pavel was at the Red Army arena. The Embassy staff rushed over there and found him. One of his legs was broken. The medical staff has done what they can, and they think he'll be stable enough to fly out tomorrow. Everyone feels the best thing now is to get him out of Russia as quickly as possible."

For the second time that day, Dmitri broke down. "How bad? How bad?"

Donny shook his head. "There's no way of knowing. But he's alive and he's coming to Canada. Dmitri, this is good news!"

"But Pavel...he loves so much hockey. And he loves Russia, and now he has lost both." Dmitri sank into a chair and covered his face with his hands. Donny motioned for Maggie and Gary to follow him into the kitchen.

"He needs some time to take all of this in. It's a lot for someone to go through in just a few days," their father sighed. "I don't know what to say, you two. I'm so proud of how you've handled all of this."

"But I feel so bad for Dmitri!" Maggie exclaimed.

Her father nodded. "The best thing we can do is to help him and his family find a good life here."

"At least they're away from all of that crime!" Gary said.

"Well, we're not perfect either," his father reminded him. Gary thought about Justin and the steroids, and Rob Duffy. "But yes, we are lucky to live in Canada."

Gary walked through the living room on his way to bed. The solitary figure of Dmitri sat in the darkness, staring out of the window.

20 THE WAITING GAME

THE NEXT DAY, the MacDonalds tried to stick to their daily routine, but everyone was distracted by the events of the night before. Dmitri's mother and Tatiana would not arrive at the Charlottetown airport until early evening. In the meantime, Dmitri had to go to practice. Donny agreed to let Gary and Maggie take the day off school so they could all go to the rink together.

"I think he's going to need all of us there today," Donny suggested, remembering how tired Dmitri had looked at breakfast, with dark bags under his eyes. He'd pushed his food around his plate but hadn't eaten anything.

"I have some good news for you, Dmitri," Donny said as they all piled into the minivan. "The police in Albuquerque picked up Vladimir Smolikin late last night. He's in custody and they're ready to start deportation procedures against him."

"It is too late though, I think," Dmitri replied solemnly. He stared out the window as they started the drive to the Civic Centre. Gary was surprised when his dad parked behind the building and led them up a sidewalk to the back door. "The cameras will be waiting for us out front," his dad said grimly.

As soon as they walked into the rink, Gunner and Dave Anderson came rushing up to Dmitri. Anderson grabbed the young Russian in a bear hug.

"Hang in there, kid," the red-headed coach said, slapping him on the back. "We're all rooting for ya."

"I've got an extra set of gear waiting for you," the trainer added eagerly. "I heard that you left yours in New Mexico."

"Thank you," Dmitri said softly. Then he paused and turned back to his coach. "The boys on the team…they are angry with me?"

Dave Anderson shook his head. "Kid, everyone knows what you've been going through. This is big-time stuff. Don't let a couple of knuckleheads in the media put you off your game. What matters now is that your family is safe, and you're back with the team, where you belong."

Dmitri didn't look convinced, but he followed the old trainer down the hallway to pick up his gear. Dave Anderson turned to the MacDonalds.

"You've been a great help. Donny, is it?" Dave Anderson shook Donny's hand.

"These are my children, Maggie and Gary." They also shook hands with the Snow Dogs' coach.

"Gary. Don't you play for the Abbies? I think I've seen you in practice a couple of times. You're a good little player," Anderson said. Gary felt himself blushing and hoped his sister hadn't noticed. The Coach excused himself, grabbed his stick and gloves and headed out onto the ice.

"Nice compliment," Maggie teased. "The Snow Dogs' coach thinks you're a 'good little hockey player.'"

Gary had cringed slightly at the word "little," but he was

too pleased to really mind his sister's ribbing. Their dad went off to make some phone calls and Gary and Maggie climbed up into the stands to watch the practice.

A large group of reporters was hovering in the hallway between the dressing room and the Zamboni entrance to the ice. As soon as Dmitri stepped out of the locker room, they swarmed around him. Darby Sanders stepped in between the cameras and Dmitri and helped his teammate onto the ice. Gary saw Darby whisper something to Dmitri, and for the first time in days, Dmitri cracked a smile.

Gary enjoyed every minute of the practice. He kept his eyes glued on Dmitri, watching his every move. The Russian was even faster and smoother than he had been at the beginning of the season when they had first met. His time in the NHL had obviously pushed his play up to another level. Gary marvelled at Dmitri's every twist and turn, moves that casually left even experienced players like Darby Sanders lagging behind.

During a break in the action, Gary looked around the arena. The media horde was busy recording Dmitri's every move. Some of the reporters were familiar; others weren't. Gary figured they were from off the Island and had flown in specifically to follow Dmitri's story. The out-of-town reporters weren't the only unfamiliar faces. Gary also noticed a couple of conspicuous-looking men with bulging suit jackets and earphones. It was nice to know that the RCMP was keeping an eye on his friend.

After practice, the Snow Dogs held a news conference. Dmitri stood uncomfortably beside Clark Dinsmore. The Russian's hair was still wet from the shower, and he looked young and vulnerable now that he was off the ice. Dinsmore clearly answered questions about where Dmitri had been and what was going on with his contract.

"I repeat…Mr. Rushkov is pleased to be back with the Snow Dogs organization. The news about Mr. Rushkov demanding a contract for his brother was a misunderstanding. All contract disputes have now been resolved to the mutual satisfaction of both parties," Dinsmore announced. The reporters simultaneously shouted questions at the team president.

Maggie elbowed Gary. "Did you hear that? Why didn't he explain that the mafia made Dmitri do it?"

"I heard Dad talking to Dinsmore on the phone. He said the RCMP suggested it would be safer for Dmitri if the mafia was kept out of it," Gary explained.

Maggie shushed him as Dmitri took his place in front of the microphones.

"I am very happy to be back with my team, the Snow Dogs. I have most respect for the Snow Dogs organization and Mr. Dinsmore. I want to thank everyone who has helped me through this difficult time, especially the MacDonald family." Dmitri looked over to where Gary and Maggie were standing and gave them a brief smile. "I look forward to returning to New Mexico whenever team needs me," Dmitri concluded.

The reporters tried to ask more questions but Clark Dinsmore waved them off, directing Dmitri back to the locker room.

Gary and Maggie were on their way to the back door to meet their dad when they almost bumped into a reporter and cameraperson leaving the rink.

"It could just be a big publicity stunt," the reporter said as they rushed past the MacDonalds. "I wouldn't put it past Dinsmore."

"Yeah, well, dream on, buddy. It's going to take more than a pouty Russian to get the crowds back to watch this team. The Snow Dogs are going nowhere," the cameraperson replied in a sarcastic voice.

"Oh yeah, they're going somewhere alright," the reporter laughed. "Right out of town."

Gary and Maggie exchanged confused looks. What were they talking about?

They reached the back door to wait for their dad. The door to the Snow Dogs' locker room was open, and just inside, Darby Sanders was having a heated argument with Dave Anderson.

"Can't you push them for some more talent? Ask Dinsmore now while he's here and in a good mood. If we don't get some more offence, we're finished. And if we don't start winning…" Sanders didn't finish his sentence.

"Dinsmore's only concern is winning in New Mexico. That's where the owners are and, believe me, they're breathing down his neck." For a minute, nobody spoke. "Darby, you've been around the farm team long enough to know how this works. Rushkov's a star. We're lucky if we get to keep him for a game or two. But we're not keeping him for good. And we're not going to get any more help."

Darby Sanders walked out of the locker room, shaking his head.

Gary waited for Darby to leave the building. He wanted to ask Maggie what she thought about the discussions they'd just overheard. But he didn't get a chance. A moment later, Donny MacDonald appeared from the dressing room, followed by Dmitri.

"Time to get our media superstar home," Donny teased. Dmitri smiled, looking much more relaxed now that the media conference was over.

"This day takes so long," Dmitri said as they drove home. "It is still so many hours until Tatiana and my mother arrive."

"And Pavel," Donny added. "We were able to get him on a flight from Moscow that connected in London. Your mother and Tatiana were already there. We thought it would be better if they all flew to Canada together."

Dmitri turned to look out the window, though Gary noticed him wipe his hand across his face. "They still arrive tonight?"

Donny nodded. "Nine-forty-five flight from Halifax. Think you can hold on till then?"

"I have practice tonight," Gary reminded his father. "But I'll be done in plenty of time to go to the airport, right?"

"Maybe I come to your practice?" Dmitri asked.

"I think it's better you keep a low profile for now," Donny replied. "Another time."

Gary tried not to look disappointed. It would have been so cool to have Dmitri at practice!

"By the way, Dmitri, we've got a house for you and your family to stay in,"

Donny continued. "It's small, but at least it's a place of your own. For as long as you want it."

"A house? All for us?" Dmitri caught his breath.

"It's just tiny. Three bedrooms, a kitchen. Nice backyard, though, with room for a garden."

"In Russia, we always live in apartment, sometimes sharing with other families. But a house? Never."

"Maybe an apartment would be better?" Donny asked, looking concerned.

Dmitri shook his head. "No. This will make my mother very happy. Finally, after so many years, her own garden. And her own house. She will not believe such luck."

Gary smiled at his friend's enthusiastic response. He wondered what the Russians would think of his own big, old, three-storey Victorian home. He realized again how different his life had been from Dmitri and Pavel's.

Later that afternoon, the Canadian Embassy called from London with an update on the Rushkovs' trip. As planned, the women had been reunited with Pavel.

"We had a doctor out at the airport to check on Pavel's leg. They had to give him some painkillers, but he's doing okay. He'll be walking again in no time, Dmitri," Donny reassured the young Russian, who still looked anxious.

"But hockey?"

Donny shrugged. "Only time will tell. And remember, it's safer for you and your family if the story of Pavel's beating never gets out."

Dmitri looked troubled, but nodded his agreement. Not long after, the Russian excused himself and went to his room to prepare for his family's arrival.

ARRIVALS **21**

AFTER SUPPER, Donny drove Gary to his practice. Gary was surprised when his father parked the minivan and got out.

"You don't have to stay, Dad. It's just a practice. I'm sure you've got lots to do," Gary urged.

"I'd just end up pacing around the house like everyone else. All I can do now is wait. This will help the time go by," his dad smiled.

Gary's good mood faded when he walked into the dressing room. The first thing he saw was Justin Johnston, lacing up his skates. Gary went as far down the bench from Justin as he could. He started unpacking his hockey gear, and tried to avoid looking in his teammate's direction.

"Aren't you going to ask me what I'm doing here, MacWuss?" Justin's voice boomed through the locker room. Gary looked around anxiously but none of the coaches were on hand. He ignored Justin's question and continued to dress for practice. "I'm talking to you, you little punk," Justin growled, walking in Gary's direction.

The door swung open and Coach Mulligan entered the room. The Coach had been working his players hard since his return. Nothing more had been said about his angry departure, but he'd made it clear to the boys that he wasn't going to tolerate any more shenanigans from this team. The Coach cleared his throat. "Boys, as you can see, Justin Johnston is back in the lineup. I'd like to put all of this behind us and concentrate on winning hockey games. That's all I've got to say on the subject, and I don't want to hear another word about it from any of you either." He glared in Justin's direction and gave Gary a meaningful look as well.

Russ stuck his head in the door. "Five minutes," he said.

All through practice, Gary tried to stay away from Justin. But it seemed like the older boy was intent on nudging and elbowing Gary every chance he got.

"Why doesn't he leave me alone?" Gary whispered to Todd as they collected the pucks out of the goal.

"He's telling everyone that this whole thing was your fault because you snitched on him," Todd whispered back. "I'd keep an eye on him."

At the end of practice, Coach Mulligan gathered the boys around in the locker room. "Okay, here are the lines. Manning, MacDonald, Johnston. You're number one. I'm counting on you to get the puck in the net. We've only got a couple of weeks before the playoffs and I want your line to be running like a well-oiled machine by then. Am I clear?"

Gary ripped off his gear and threw it in his bag as fast as he could. He wanted to get out of the arena before Justin had a chance to get changed. As he was about to leave the locker room, Johnston stepped out of the showers. He grabbed Gary by the jacket and dragged him into the shower area.

"Last chance, MacWuss. You mess with me once more and you'll never play hockey again. Got it?" Justin hissed. He leaned forward as if preparing to push Gary against the hard shower wall. "Wouldn't want to hit that delicate head of yours, would we? Watch your back, MacWuss."

He shoved Gary back into the locker room and walked away. Gary looked around the room to see if anyone had noticed. His teammates were all busy, getting changed and packing up their gear. No one seemed willing to meet his gaze. Gary shook his head and walked out the door.

ON THE DRIVE HOME, Gary tried to decide whether or not he should tell his father about what had happened. He didn't want to be a snitch. And he *certainly* didn't want to do anything else to aggravate Justin.

"Justin's back," he finally said, as if it were no big deal.

"Coach Mulligan told me. Apparently, the team made a deal with Justin's dad. He'd drop the court case in exchange for Justin getting back on the team," Donny explained.

"How is that fair?" Gary cried.

"It's not. But I guess the team didn't want this thing to get into the papers. They decided to make the whole thing go away." Donny paused. "I'm sorry, Gary. I really am."

"Now Justin will be able to do whatever he wants," Gary said, thinking of the scene in the locker room.

"I don't think so. Justin's dad is not too pleased with his son right now. I think Justin will stay on the straight and narrow."

"You don't know Justin."

"What does that mean?"

"Oh, never mind." Gary slumped down in his seat and stared out the window. As far as he could tell, there was only one good thing about the whole situation: Justin was in his second year of bantam. Next year, he would move up and Gary and Todd would have the team to themselves. But the rest of this season was another story.

AT AROUND NINE O'CLOCK, Dmitri insisted that they go to the airport.

"But it's only ten minutes away," Maggie protested.

"I must be there," Dmitri said stubbornly. Gary smiled and went to get his jacket. When he returned, Dmitri was standing in the doorway, clutching two enormous bundles of flowers and balloons.

"You think it is too much?" he asked anxiously. Gary gave him a thumbs-up and his friend grinned.

When they arrived at the Charlottetown airport, the MacDonalds, Lisa, and Dmitri were escorted by an airport security guard to a wood-panelled room. Donny explained that they would wait here until the plane landed.

Gary went out to the waiting area to check the flight arrivals for what felt like the millionth time. Lisa was just finishing up a call on her cellphone. She came and stood next to him, and for a moment, they both just stared at the arrivals board. Gary thought about how hard she had worked on Dmitri's behalf, and about how much happier his dad seemed these days. "I'm sorry I was so mean to you. Before," he said shyly, still staring at the list of arrivals.

Lisa smiled at him. "It's okay," she said. "It's tough to see your family changing like that. My parents split up when I was twelve. So I can kind of relate to what you're going through." Suddenly, her smile changed to a full-fledged grin.

"Besides, I'm a lawyer. I'm used to people being mean to me."

"You want to play shinny some time?" Gary asked, finally turning and looking her in the eye.

"When we're finished dodging the Russian mafia and the TV cameras, sure," Lisa smiled. She pointed him back toward the wood-panelled room.

"I think they bought it." Lisa winked at Donny as she and Gary rejoined the others.

"Bought what?" Maggie asked.

"Cheryl Porter sent out a news release saying that Dmitri was en route back to Albuquerque. So we're hoping the media will be so busy watching for him there, that we'll have some peace and quiet here."

"Am I going back to New Mexico?" Dmitri asked.

"It looks that way. Dinsmore said you could have a couple of days here to get your family settled. But I guess they'd like you back in New Mexico for next week's home games," Donny replied. "I hope that's alright, Dmitri. I know this has been a lot to go through."

"Will Dmitri play Saturday night for Charlottetown?" Gary asked his dad.

"I guess that's up to Dmitri."

The Russian immediately gave Gary a thumbs-up.

"Cool!" Gary exclaimed. "And your mom, Tatiana, and Pavel will be able to watch!"

THERE WAS A KNOCK on the door. "Plane's on final approach," the security guard told them. He handed each of them a neon-coloured security badge. "Put these on and I'll take you out through the baggage area. Nice and private."

The group tried to look inconspicuous as they walked past the baggage handlers. There were only a few people working, and no one seemed to notice the NHL player and his friends walking by even though Gary and Maggie each carried a bunch of flowers and balloons.

"I feel like an idiot," Gary whispered to his sister. They both giggled.

"I can't wait to see them," she said as they stood amidst the luggage trolleys.

The security guard led Dmitri and Donny out onto the tarmac.

"This is so exciting," Lisa said. The door to the baggage area opened and two RCMP officers joined them.

"Did you want us out on the tarmac, Ms. McCulloch?" asked one of the officers.

"No, let's give them some space. They'll need to get used to having you guys around," Lisa replied. "I think the police make them a little nervous in Russia."

A few minutes later, there was a gust of cold wind and snow as the large door opened. A flight attendant pushed a wheelchair into the baggage room. Gary stared into the face of a darker version of Dmitri. Pavel's face was haggard and bruised, but there was no mistaking the younger brother. He wore a large plastic cast and his leg was stretched out awkwardly in front of him.

"You Gary," he said, offering his hand from beneath a woollen blanket. "I Pavel."

The two shook hands as the door opened again. This time, Dmitri came in with his arm around the shoulder of a tiny woman wearing a handkerchief on her head. She looked like a wizened old elf next to her muscular son.

"*Dobre, dobre*," she said, brushing snow off Pavel, as Donny and Tatiana entered. So this was Dmitri's girlfriend! Gary couldn't take his eyes off her. She was as tall as Dmitri and even more beautiful than in her pictures. Dmitri wrapped his arm around her shoulders and she snuggled into his jacket, her long, blonde hair almost hiding the tears that were streaming down her face.

Gary stood, shyly holding the flowers and balloons. Finally, Tatiana broke free from Dmitri's embrace and came over to where Gary was standing. She grabbed him in a hug and kissed him on the top of his head. "You are a good friend to my Dmitri," she said.

"And thanks to you, too." She shook hands with Maggie, who handed her the flowers and balloons.

Gary gave his bouquet to Dmitri's mother. "Baba," she said pointing to herself. "Baba."

Gary looked at Dmitri for an explanation. "She's saying she is like your grandmother now," Dmitri explained. "She told me she feels like you are our family."

After even more introductions and hugs all around, Donny and the RMCP officers huddled near the door. "We're going to bring the cars around to an entrance back here," Donny explained. "We can get on our way without going back into the terminal."

Tatiana looked concerned. "Why are the police here? I thought there was nothing left to fear."

"We're just being careful, ma'am," one of the officers

explained. "We just want to be sure the situation is totally under control before we lighten up on our surveillance."

"Tatiana, it's okay. You are in North America now," Dmitri said.

"Canada good," Pavel said, wincing slightly as the attendant wheeled him toward the door.

"Yes, Canada is good," Donny echoed. Gary hoped he was right.

DMITRI'S FUTURE 22

THE NEXT DAY AT SCHOOL, everyone peppered Gary with questions about Dmitri. A picture of the MacDonalds' house had appeared on the front page of the sports section, next to a photo of Dmitri at practice. Now everyone wanted to know where Dmitri was.

"So, is he in New Mexico?" Todd asked, getting his books out of his locker.

"He's still here," Gary whispered to his friend. "I'll tell you more later." Gary felt badly about keeping Todd in the dark, but there had been too many people hovering around their lockers and the last thing Dmitri needed was more trouble.

AFTER SCHOOL, Gary and Todd walked over to the house where Dmitri and his family were staying. Dmitri answered the door and gave Gary a big hug. He shook Todd's hand enthusiastically and then made introductions.

Pavel was lying on the couch with a large blanket spread over his cast. Todd looked surprised to see the young Russian's injuries. Baba Rushkov insisted on making tea and cookies, and Tatiana dashed in and out of the room, carrying cups and plates for everyone. Dmitri sat in the middle of it all, a grin permanently stuck on his face.

"Finally, the Snow Dogs agree to let me play tomorrow. Now, my family, they all come to game," Dmitri explained. "You boys come too, I think?"

"Yeah, my entire family's coming," Gary replied.

"The team is not so happy with me playing. But when I say I want to thank Charlottetown people for so helping me and my family, they agree," Dmitri continued.

"Why don't they want you to play?" Todd asked.

"They want me go to New Mexico right away. But I go Monday. I must see my family first," Dmitri grinned over at his brother. "My mama and Tatiana must take care of this big baby, my brother Pavel. He such bad motorcycle driver," Dmitri explained to Todd. When Todd wasn't looking, he gave Gary a quick wink.

Gary noticed that Pavel was straining to follow their conversation. He could tell that the young Russian wanted to be able to understand them. Gary glanced over at a pile of hockey magazines on the table in front of Pavel.

"I like pictures hockey," Pavel laughed, noticing where Gary was looking. "I no read. But good pictures."

Gary picked up the latest edition of *The Hockey News*. Rob Duffy's name was mentioned on the cover. Gary flipped through the pages, looking for the article.

"Hey, look at this!" he exclaimed. "Duffy's now the big enforcer for Tampa Bay."

"Oh yeah, I remember hearing something about that," Todd said. "Didn't he have some kind of record in penalty minutes in the International League? Tampa decided to call him up to protect Brad Richards. He was getting a lot of goals, but the other teams were starting to go after him too much. Now Duffy's there to protect him."

Dmitri shook his head. "It makes me mad, these players like Duffy. Why we need such protection? Why we can't just play hockey?"

"Brad's a pretty small guy for the NHL," Gary pointed out. Richards had grown up on PEI, and he was the hero of many of the young Island players. "But you're right, Dmitri. It's too bad you can't just concentrate on playing."

"My brother big guy in head," Pavel said, eager to jump into the conversation. They all laughed and Pavel smiled at his first joke in English.

LATER THAT EVENING, over dinner, Gary asked a question that had been bugging him all day long. "Dad, why don't the Snow Dogs want Dmitri to play? He's their star player!"

"I think they're worried that having Dmitri here for one game will just point out how bad the rest of the team really is," Maggie suggested.

Donny nodded. "You may be right," he said. "By the way, your mother called to ask if you two were going to spend the weekend there. Oh... and she has some extra towels and stuff to take over to Dmitri's house. You can do that tomorrow."

"What about the game?" Gary asked.

"Your mom thought we could all go together. Maybe go out for pizza beforehand. A little family celebration," Donny explained.

After their father left the room, Gary looked at his sister, confused.

"Did he say go out together—as a family?" Gary asked. "What's up with that?"

Maggie shrugged. "I guess everyone's finally learning to get along. But I don't think it means 'together' together, if that's what you're thinking."

"No, I wasn't even thinking that," Gary admitted. "Is that bad?"

His sister smiled. "No, I think that's good. I mean, I miss being a family sometimes. But other times, I'm just happy that there's no more fighting. I couldn't stand all the arguing."

"Yeah, I know what you mean," Gary nodded. "I remember you used to say it would be better if they were both happy. I guess you were right."

"Are you actually admitting that I was right about something?" his sister teased.

As he lay in bed that night, Gary thought about his conversation with his sister. Had he finally accepted that his parents were split up for good? He felt a surge of conflicting emotions. Did he still want them back together? What about his mom and Mr. Doucette? They seemed to be getting along well. And Lisa was even staying over at their house now, especially with everything that had been going on. As he drifted off to sleep, he wondered what Lisa would think of the MacDonalds going out together as a family. He hoped she wouldn't mind.

CHANGES **23**

GARY CAME DOWNSTAIRS for breakfast on Saturday to find his father fuming over something in the paper.

"What is it, Dad?" Gary asked sleepily as he poured himself some cereal and milk.

"The Snow Dogs have changed their minds. Now they're saying Dmitri can't play tonight. The local media are ripping into Dmitri, blaming him. But Anderson says it was New Mexico's call. They don't want to risk him getting hurt," Donny growled. "This is definitely not the kind of PR the Charlottetown Snow Dogs are looking for."

Gary took the paper and started reading. "But Dmitri said he wanted to play."

"Well, I'm afraid it's not up to him," his father replied. "Whatever New Mexico wants, New Mexico gets. You should know that by now. Anyway, the problem is bigger than Dmitri," Donny continued. "I mean, this columnist is right, it just doesn't make sense. The Snow Dogs may have to pull out of Charlottetown because of low attendance at the games. Yet if they would let Dmitri play tonight, they'd have a sell-out crowd."

"Do you really think they are going to pull out? After just

one year?" Gary asked quietly, not sure he wanted to hear the answer.

His father sighed. "You know, at one point I was trying to track down Clark Dinsmore to work out a deal for Dmitri. His office gave me a phone number somewhere in Louisiana. I later heard that he was just outside of New Orleans, where they've just built a brand new twenty-thousand-seat arena."

"But a farm team would never attract twenty thousand people!" Gary exclaimed.

"Maybe not here—this is a small market," said his dad. But this suburb has over a million people, with a couple of million more within an easy drive. Granted, they don't know much about hockey. But this is the way the NHL is heading."

"But Louisiana? They don't even have snow!"

"I know, Gary. But look at where the Snow Dogs are based. They don't have snow in New Mexico either."

Later that afternoon, Gary and Todd were playing shinny in the backyard. It was one of those crisp, sunny afternoons when the ice glistened under their skates and their breath swirled around them like tiny clouds.

"I don't think places like Louisiana should even be allowed to get hockey teams," Todd argued. "What do they know about hockey? No one down there even plays!"

"And they could never have a backyard rink," Gary joked.

"They'd have to build a dome over their yards," Todd snickered. Then he grew serious again. "I hope your dad's wrong. I just wish more people would come out to the Snow Dogs' games."

"They would have come tonight. But they'll probably just stay home now that Dmitri's not going to play," Gary said, slapping a puck against the boards. It gave a dull thud and spun back toward him. He flipped it effortlessly to his friend, who raced to the net and slipped it in.

A few hours later, Gary, Maggie, and their father sat at the pizza place waiting for their mother to arrive. She was about ten minutes late and breathless by the time she joined them at the table.

"Darrell and I just dropped some linens and towels over to Dmitri's house. And that delightful old woman insisted that we sit down and have tea. I didn't want to offend her, but now I'm running a little late." Martha MacDonald paused to catch her breath and smiled over at her children.

"When are they heading over to the game?" Maggie asked as her mother scanned the menu.

Her mother shrugged. "Well, I guess they're not going now. Dmitri caught a flight to New Mexico a couple of hours ago. A last-minute change of plans."

Gary looked at his mother. "Dmitri's gone?" She nodded.

Donny sighed. "This is not going to go over well with the crowd. I guess I was hoping the Snow Dogs would change their minds once they figured out what a public relations disaster this was going to be."

"Let's have a toast anyway!" Martha said, cheerfully raising her water glass. "To Dmitri and his family, safe and sound in Canada!" The MacDonalds clinked glasses.

"Well, I guess we may as well tell you our news," Donny said, looking over at Martha, who nodded. "We wanted the two of you to know that we are officially filing for divorce. We don't want either of you to worry about it. It's no big deal, just some paperwork. But we wanted you to know."

Gary didn't say a word. He snuck a glance at his sister. She was busy playing with her napkin. For a minute or two, no one spoke.

"What we're trying to say is…we think this is for the best. For everyone. And look," Martha paused to smile at Donny, "I think we're getting along better now than we have for a while."

The waiter came by to take their order, interrupting any further discussion. Gary sat there, trying to figure out what he was feeling. Dmitri had left without saying goodbye, and that was bad enough. His parents' news just added to his disappointment. For a while now, he'd known that his parents weren't getting back together. Still, he was sad as he realized this was one of the last times they'd be together as a family.

"You know, this is a good idea," Donny said as they munched on their garlic sticks. "Maybe we can make this a regular thing. A family supper every once in a while."

"But does it always have to be pizza?" Maggie teased.

"We'll still be a family," Martha reassured them, laughing. "That will never change."

Gary swallowed hard. He tried to think about Dmitri and his family, and what they were doing right now. Then he remembered that his friend was gone.

"You know, I don't really feel like going to the game," Gary said.

His parents and Maggie looked surprised.

"Can I still go?" Maggie asked. "And can I have your tickets?" She smiled apologetically at her brother. "I mean it's one of the last games of the season and some of my friends want to go."

"Fine by me," Donny said.

"I think I'll just head home after dinner, too," Martha added. "One more ticket for you, Maggie."

Later, as the MacDonalds left the restaurant, Gary couldn't shake the feeling that something had ended. But when he noticed his mother looking at him with concern, he was able to smile back for the first time this winter.

THE SPORTS SECTION of Monday's *Guardian* was filled with stories of Dmitri's no-show. The reporter mentioned that Dmitri's family had arrived from Russia and speculated that they wanted to get their hands on his NHL salary. Perhaps they had pushed him to go to New Mexico, he said. There were also comments from fans, angry that the young Russian hadn't been in the lineup.

"We can still make the playoffs if the fans stick with us," Darby Sanders was quoted as saying. "And if New Mexico would give us a couple of good players, hey, we might even win this thing."

Gary suspected that Darby's comments wouldn't go over too well with the Snow Dogs' management. However, it appeared the captain wasn't the only person mad at the team. The local radio call-in show was filled with irate fans asking why the Snow Dogs had sent Dmitri back to New Mexico so soon. Gary felt sorry for Dave Anderson, who was in the studio talking to the callers. He was stuck trying to defend the decision, even though Gary knew that he, too, wanted the team to get some better players.

"I'm not going to renew my season tickets if this contin-ues," one fan shouted through the phone line.

"Let's face it. If you don't make the playoffs, the team is toast here in Charlottetown," another suggested.

"I don't think that's true," Dave Anderson jumped in. "Clark Dinsmore is very committed to keeping the Snow Dogs here on the Island. He has told me as much."

"Would you put your job on the line if they said they were going to move the team?" the caller persisted.

"Uh, I'd have to think about that," Anderson replied. "But it's not an issue."

Listening to the callers, Gary wondered if Dave Anderson was telling the truth.

THE ENFORCER 24

THE NEXT COUPLE OF WEEKS were a blur of exams and hockey for Gary and Todd. Meanwhile, Pavel's recovery continued. The cast was taken off the first week of March, and he was able to hobble around the Civic Centre, leaning on a cane for support. Socky Mulligan, back on the job after his accident at Christmas, had befriended Pavel. He even promised to teach Pavel to drive the Zamboni once his leg got a little stronger. Socky said he had a job for Pavel at the arena, if the young Russian wanted it.

Dmitri continued to shine with New Mexico, and there were rumblings that he could be named rookie of the year. However, some commentators, including Bobby Dawson, continued to lobby against him.

"How can you reward a kid who takes off in the middle of the season, just because he didn't like his contract?" Dawson sneered. "Nah, this guy's a whiner, and probably a flash in the pan. We'll see how he does next season."

With everything that was going on, Gary and Todd didn't have many chances to visit with Dmitri's family. So finally, Tatiana put her foot down and insisted the boys come over on Saturday night for dinner—and to watch the Snow Dogs on *Hockey Night in Canada.*

"Baba wanted to make you a traditional Russian meal with borscht and perogies," Tatiana explained as the boys settled on the couch beside Pavel.

"Borscht?" Todd asked politely.

"How you say—beet soup," Tatiana explained.

"No worry," Pavel interrupted. "I say we eat pizza." Just then, Baba came into the room, carrying a pizza box and shaking her head. Everyone laughed. It was such a contradictory picture: the old Russian woman in her babushka, as they called the handkerchief on her head, wearing two bulky sweaters and an apron, and carrying a pizza box.

The Snow Dogs were playing the Tampa Bay Lightning and during the warm-up Gary noticed the familiar figure of Rob Duffy.

"Oh no," Gary moaned, pointing at the television. "I forgot Duffy was playing for them." He explained to Tatiana and Pavel who Duffy was.

On Dmitri's first shift, the Tampa Bay coach quickly changed his lines and Rob Duffy came jumping over the boards. "They're trying to put Duffy on Dmitri," Todd explained. "They want to make sure Dmitri doesn't score."

Rob Duffy was like Dmitri's shadow as the Russian tried to break into the Lightning's zone. When Dmitri finally did manage to break free for a few seconds, Duffy hooked him from behind. The referee instantly blew his whistle and directed Duffy to the penalty box. But as Duffy skated past Dmitri, he elbowed him in the stomach. Dmitri doubled over, holding his stomach, as his teammates swarmed around the Tampa defender.

"What a goon!" Todd yelled at the TV.

"What is 'goon'?" Pavel asked.

"It's someone who...who does that!" Gary exclaimed. "Someone who's better at fighting than hockey."

"I do not like these goons," Tatiana said angrily. "In Russia, we do not have players who are there just to pick fights. Our coaches would dismiss such a player."

She glanced over at Baba who was watching from the kitchen doorway. Tatiana went over and said something to her in Russian in a soothing voice. Baba took a tissue from her sleeve and dabbed her eyes before heading back into the kitchen.

"It is sometimes better for her not to watch, I think," Tatiana explained, gripping the arm of the chair with her nails as the trainer helped Dmitri off the ice.

Dmitri played sporadically in the first period but seemed better when the teams came back out. About halfway through the second period he scored; a few minutes later, he assisted on another. By the time the period ended the Snow Dogs had pulled into a 2–1 lead. Things continued to go well until midway through the third period. Dmitri was on the ice when he noticed Duffy coming over the boards. He looked over at the bench, as if asking to come off, but the coaches waved him back to the faceoff circle.

"Now we see," Pavel said, banging his cane on the floor. "You no touch my brother." Tatiana waved at him to keep his voice down, and Pavel snapped back at her in Russian.

"Look!" Gary interrupted their argument. Duffy was chasing after Dmitri. Just as he got his stick on the Russian player, one of the Snow Dogs crashed into the Lightning enforcer. Duffy's stick jabbed up underneath Dmitri's face guard. Tatiana screamed in horror as blood spurted from Dmitri's face onto the ice. It took the trainer and medical staff more than five minutes to stop the bleeding. The announcers said that the cut was just above Dmitri's eye.

"Any lower and that could have been a career-ending injury," one of the commentators pointed out.

The crowd at the rink in Florida rose to give Dmitri a standing ovation as he was guided off the ice, a towel covering most of his face.

"He'll be heading to the hospital to stitch that one up," the announcers concluded.

Tatiana got up and went to turn off the television.

"No, wait!" Gary urged her. "Look, they're talking to the League Commissioner. He's at the game."

They turned up the sound as the reporter asked the Commissioner about possible sanctions against Rob Duffy.

"We'll have a full investigation into the matter," the Commissioner said, looking into the camera. "I must say I was sickened by what I saw tonight. This just strengthens my resolve to clean up this kind of dirty play in the NHL."

"Yeah, right," Todd sneered. "He always says that, but they never do a thing."

Later as Gary and Todd were getting ready to leave, the phone rang. Tatiana answered it and immediately waved for the boys to stop. She spoke quickly in Russian. It was obviously Dmitri. She paused for a moment to translate.

"It is Dmitri. He is fine. He is finished at hospital." She listened again. "He has fifteen stitches but his eye is not hurt. Just…swelling," she continued. "Dmitri says…his team will ask for this player to be suspended for rest of season." She continued to talk to Dmitri in Russian and then paused and smiled before hanging up the phone.

"He says all will be okay," she blushed. Pavel nodded and gave her a thumbs-up.

BEFORE GARY went to bed, he stopped in the living room where his dad and Lisa were watching a movie. His dad paused the film.

"What's up?" Donny asked. He and Lisa had also been watching the game and were concerned about the attack on Dmitri.

"Duffy's going to be really mad at Dmitri," Gary's voice was filled with concern for his friend. "Do you think he'll hurt Dmitri again the next time they play?"

"You know, I feel badly for Duffy," his dad said. "I don't think he meant to hurt Dmitri as much as he did. But from what the commentators were saying, Duffy's NHL career is over. He already had a bad reputation because of all the stuff that went on here. I think he's back in the minors for good. No team can risk having this kind of bad PR."

"I was kind of embarrassed," Gary said, his face grim. "We made such a big deal about how great it is to live in North America and how much safer it is than Russia. And then Dmitri gets beat up by Duffy the same way Pavel got hurt by the Russian mafia."

"At least you don't have to worry about that on the Abbies!"

Lisa smiled. Gary wasn't so sure. But he still wasn't ready to tell his dad about Justin's threats. He didn't want to be a snitch—not after what had happened with the pills. He'd just have to hope the season would be over before Justin was able to make his move.

THE PLAYOFFS . . . OR ELSE 25

DMITRI'S INJURY WAS front page news on Monday. The Snow Dogs had asked that Rob Duffy be suspended for the rest of the season. Because both men had played in Charlottetown, the Island was abuzz with discussion of the attack. Some argued that Duffy's hit hadn't been intentional, and that he was taking the fall to make the Commissioner look tough on violence. Others argued that enforcers had no place in hockey.

Gary tried to put all of the NHL talk aside and focus on his own team. The Abbies had finished the season in a three-way log-jam at the top of the standings. Charlottetown, Parkdale, and Summerside all had seventy-four points. Because Summerside had won more games than the other two teams, they were declared the winners of the regular season. That led to a tough series between the Abbies and Parkdale, with the Abbies winning the fifth and deciding game in overtime. Now, battered and bruised, they were about to begin a best-of-five series against Summerside. The first game was Saturday night—at the same time as the Snow Dogs' final game of the season. By the time of their last practice on Friday night, the entire team was a bundle of nerves.

"I can't believe we're going to miss the Snow Dogs' last game," Todd said as he and Gary skated around the Civic Centre ice before practice.

"Their last game here ever," Justin skated up behind them. "What are you going to do without your beloved Snow Dogs, MacWuss? You and that good-for-nothing Russky are such good friends." Justin skated away, elbowing Gary as he went past. "Just ignore him," Todd muttered.

"I can't just let him say that stuff about Dmitri," Gary snapped back.

"Believe me, Gary, nobody listens to a word Justin says," Todd replied, rolling his eyes. The Coach blew his whistle and the team gathered at centre ice for a final pep talk.

"This is it," the Coach told them. "The whole season comes down to the next five games. I need all of you to be at the top of your games. Eat, sleep, and dream hockey. Or, better yet, dream about winning."

ON SATURDAY NIGHT, the Summerside stadium was jammed to the rafters. The fans booed loudly as the Abbies skated onto the ice for their warm-up. Gary scanned the stands, looking for his parents. His mom, Darrell, and Maggie were sitting in the small section of the arena set aside for the Abbies' fans. But his dad and Lisa were nowhere in sight.

Gary's hands were shaking as the teams lined up for the opening faceoff. But he was soon caught up in the game and forgot about the fans and his nerves. The first and second periods were jam-packed with fast, fair play. When the buzzer sounded at the end of forty minutes, neither team had managed a goal.

"Those were some great saves!" Gary congratulated Billy Gaudet, the Abbies' goalie, back in the dressing room.

"Too bad you're not doing your part, MacWuss!" Justin taunted.

"Well, I don't see you scoring any hat tricks," Gary sniped back.

"You're as bad as that pathetic Russian," Justin sneered. "Did you hear his latest stupidity? That snob tried to sit in the stands and watch his team go down in flames! What a jerk. The crowd booed him because he thinks he's too big to play for the team in Charlottetown now that he's a star in New Mexico!"

Gary gave Justin a surprised look. Dmitri in Charlottetown? It didn't make any sense. Mike Bartlett walked past. "It doesn't matter what the Russky does anyway. The Snow Dogs are history. I bet the moving vans are already packing up."

"The Snow Dogs' game isn't over yet," Gary said defensively, looking at the clock on the wall of the dressing room.

"It's 8–2, MacWuss," snorted Mike. "The Snow Dogs are done."

GARY TRIED TO GET TODD'S attention as they headed out onto the ice for the third period, but Todd was busy talking to Russ. Gary wondered if Justin had made up his story. It was just too crazy to be true: Dmitri, sitting in the stands, being booed by the crowd? Up in the stands, he noticed his dad and Lisa talking to some of the Abbies' fans. It looked as if the two of them had just arrived. Gary's dad waved, though he had a sombre expression on his face.

Summerside won the opening faceoff and steamed down the ice, taking a quick shot on Gaudet, who juggled the puck and then seemed to lose his balance. Todd scrambled to grab the puck before it crossed the line. Instead he batted it into the net. The Summerside crowd went wild. Gary skated over and tapped the pads of the dejected goalie. "We'll get it right back," he told Billy.

But the Summerside defence shut down the Abbies' top scoring line. Every time Gary had the puck, he had a pair of Summerside players breathing down his neck. With less than a minute left to play, Gary took off down his wing with the puck. He was just crossing into the Summerside zone when he caught Justin out of the corner of his eye. The Summerside players were all coming at Gary, so he snuck a neat pass between them and right onto Justin's stick.

Justin wound up to take the shot and then changed his mind. He gripped his stick to flick the puck in, but the momentary hesitation was just enough time for the Summerside goalie to lunge at him and poke away the puck. Justin went sliding into the boards as the siren sounded to signal the end of the game. Summerside had taken game one.

The Abbies stood, dejected, as the crowd went wild. Gary skated over to help Justin up, but the older boy hit at Gary's extended hand with his stick. Gary howled with pain and dropped to the ice.

"Did you see that?" Gary moaned to Todd, who had come over to help. Gary's fingers were red and throbbing. "He whacked me! Justin whacked me!"

Russ slid over beside Gary and took a quick look at his

hand. "We need to get some ice on this right away." He led Gary off to the medical room.

A few minutes later, Coach Mulligan appeared at the door. "Is he alright?" he asked anxiously. Russ nodded. "There's going to be some bad swelling and bruising, but nothing appears to be broken. Still, he'd better go for an X-ray, just to be safe."

"What happened, son?" Coach Mulligan asked. "Justin says you tripped and crashed into the boards. How did you trip?"

Gary paused for a minute. He wasn't sure what to say. If he told the truth, Justin would just deny it. "I, uh, yeah, uh, I tripped. Sorry about that pass. Maybe I should have taken the shot."

The Coach shook his head. "No, Johnston missed it. Don't let him tell you otherwise. We're just going to have to win this one the hard way." The Coach turned to his assistant coach. "Russ, can you take care of the X-ray?"

"We can handle it, Vince," Donny MacDonald stepped into the medical room. "What are you going to do to Johnston?"

The Coach looked confused. "What do you mean? For missing that shot?"

"For slashing my son. His own teammate! Didn't you see what happened?" Coach Mulligan turned to Gary. "You said you tripped. Johnston said you tripped. Is that what happened?"

Gary silently pleaded with his father to understand. He nodded.

"I will not stand for this," Donny shouted. He banged his hand on the wall. "This Johnston kid has bullied Gary since the season started. He gave him pills that could have killed him. He threatened to take the team to court. And now he's taking swings at my son. If you can't protect Gary, then I will. He's off the team until you get rid of Johnston."

"But Dad—we play again on Tuesday," Gary pleaded.

"Vince. You have until Tuesday to make up your mind." Donny grabbed Gary by his good arm. "Come with me. You can change at the hospital."

THE CHARLOTTETOWN crowd's treatment of Dmitri was the top story in the newspapers and on the sports networks across North America on Sunday. But Donny wouldn't let Gary go and see his friend.

"I don't think he wants to talk to anyone right now," he explained at breakfast when Gary asked him again about what had happened. "It was all we could do to get him out of the Civic Centre and home. He's very upset by what happened. Dmitri had the best of intentions. He had just arrived back in town and thought he'd go to the arena and cheer on his teammates. Then he gets booed by his own fans."

"My friend Angela was there," Maggie added. She passed her brother the syrup as they all paused to watch another news report about the incident. "She says the crowd was yelling stuff at Dmitri, and a couple of people even threw their programs at him."

"Luckily, Lisa and I heard what was happening on the radio and managed to get to the rink in time. It took a couple of security guards to get Dmitri out the door," Donny explained, shaking his head.

"Didn't they understand that Dmitri came home because he was injured? He has a bandage on his forehead and fifteen stitches!" Gary argued.

His father shrugged. "You're trying to apply logic to what was basically a mob mentality. The fans are angry. They've heard rumours that the team is about to leave town. They've put their hearts into supporting these guys all season. Now, they see a chance to make the playoffs with Dmitri in the lineup and he's not playing. So they react."

As upset as he was about Dmitri, Gary had his own problems to deal with. He spent the rest of Sunday trying to convince his dad to let him rejoin the Abbies. But Donny refused to discuss the matter. It looked as if Gary—and the Charlottetown Snow Dogs—were both finished for the season.

26 BRAVERY AND BETRAYAL

ON MONDAY, the entire school was talking about the Abbies' loss in game one. Justin and his friends were busy telling everyone how Gary had snitched on him. When they saw Gary and Todd getting off the bus, the older boys instantly swarmed around.

"It was just a little tap! Now his daddy won't let him play. I guess I'm going to have to win it for the Abbies," Justin bragged. "MacWuss, the big friend of Dmitri 'I Watch from the Stands' Rushkov. He doesn't have any guts either. You're a pair of wusses!"

"What's going on here?" The gym teacher, Ms. Brown, pulled aside one of Justin's buddies and made her way into the centre of the pack. Gary and Todd used the diversion to make their escape and go around to another door.

"I can't believe this," Gary muttered. His hand was wrapped in a tensor bandage and was still throbbing, even though he had taken one of the painkillers that the doctor at the hospital had given him. "My dad is furious. The Snow Dogs are out of the playoffs. And Dmitri won't talk to anyone because he's so upset about what happened at the game."

"I can't believe your dad is not going to let you play," Todd whispered as they walked into science class and took their seats. Gary winced as he tried to open his book with his bandaged hand. Even if his dad did relent and let him play on Tuesday, he wasn't sure he'd be able to grip his stick.

After school, Gary went out on the backyard rink to shoot the puck around. The warm weather had made the ice slushy and there were a few bare patches where the grass was starting to show through. He had taken off the tensor bandage and the fingers on his right hand were slightly red and swollen. He slid his hand into his glove and practised holding his stick.

"Here goes nothing," he muttered. He took a couple of shots. Eventually, he found a way to hold his stick so that it didn't hurt so much when he made contact with the puck. He was concentrating so hard that he almost didn't notice when a car pulled up and a woman in a yellow jacket leaned out the window.

"You must be Gary," she said cheerfully. "I'm Marilyn Collins, from the real estate agency in town. Your dad asked me to drop this by." She handed him an envelope.

"Great rink," she added. "This will be a big selling point, I'm sure." She gave him a cheerful wave and drove off.

Gary stood, leaning on his hockey stick, looking around the backyard. What was she talking about? Just then, his father pulled into the driveway. He looked guilty as he noticed the envelope in Gary's hand.

"Uh, I guess Marilyn Collins came by, did she? Sorry, I meant to be here," his father explained. "How's the hand?"

"What did she mean about the rink being a selling point?" Gary asked, glaring at his father. He shoved the envelope into Donny's open hand.

"I didn't mean for you to find out this way," his father sighed. "I was going to wait until this whole hockey business was over."

"Find out what?" Gary persisted.

"Your mother and I have decided to sell the house. It just makes sense, Gary. The place is too big for us now, and Maggie's going to be away at school…"

Gary dropped his stick and gloves and ran into the house, slamming the door behind him. A few minutes later, he heard the thud of the puck hitting the boards. He pushed the curtain aside angrily and looked out the window. His father was standing in the middle of the rink, in his suit and tie, overcoat, and dress shoes. He had pulled on Gary's gloves and was whacking the puck at the boards over and over and over again. Finally, he paused, and Gary saw his father wipe his face.

"Too bad," Gary muttered. "You had all winter to play."

THE NEXT DAY, the air was thick with tension at the MacDonald house. When Gary refused to talk to his dad, Maggie accused him of being unreasonable.

"I told you the house was too big," she said. It was Tuesday evening. Gary kept looking at his watch, thinking about his teammates. The game started at 7:30.

"He can't do this," Gary insisted. "I won't let him. It's bad enough he won't let me play…"

"Oh, get off it. You can't play anyway. I bet you can't even hold the stick."

"Can too. I've been practising," Gary snapped. "On our rink. You know—the one that Dad is selling."

Gary got up from the table. He went to the back door and grabbed his jacket and boots. He turned away from his sister and slammed the door shut.

GARY TRUDGED THROUGH the slushy puddles. The north wind made the misty air even colder and he started to wonder if he shouldn't just head back home. "It's only a couple of blocks more," he muttered to himself.

Gary was wet and chilled by the time he got to the Rushkovs' bungalow. Tatiana opened the door and hurried him inside.

"Gary, you look so cold," she said, running to get him a towel to dry off his face and hair.

"I find sweater for you," she added. She went down the hallway and knocked on a door. Gary heard a terse conversation in Russian and then Dmitri appeared in the hallway, with Tatiana and Pavel behind him. Gary was startled to see the swelling and bruises on the Russian player's face. One eye was still almost shut, and Dmitri seemed to be squinting angrily at Gary.

"He does not look so good," Tatiana said apologetically. She handed Gary a large sweater. Pavel pointed to it, claiming ownership, and smiled.

"Are you mad at me, Dmitri?" Gary asked.

"No, not mad at you. Just mad," Dmitri began. Gary was surprised to hear the Russian's voice shaking, as if he was about to cry.

"It is too much. I almost have eye taken out by goon. Then I come back to cheer on my team and Charlottetown people attack me. What for?" Dmitri's voice got louder and his English more slurred as he became more agitated.

"I'm sorry..." Gary started to say, but Dmitri waved his hands to cut him off.

"I must finish," Dmitri continued. "I have lost my love for hockey. But now it is my job, and I must support my family. I have brought them here. Now, I must help them."

The Russian player sank onto a couch and stared blankly at Gary. He didn't know what to say. He looked over at Tatiana, whose eyes were filled with tears. Pavel, too, looked grief-stricken.

"Is this the great Canadian hockey story?" Dmitri asked Gary, in a sarcastic tone. "No, if I was hockey hero, I would play with blinded eye. Or more better, I would hit player in face so I can be big tough guy."

"That's not what it's all about," Gary said, finally breaking his shocked silence. "You know that! You didn't go through everything you did this year just to give up. Or to hate hockey."

"He not hate hockey," Pavel jumped in, waving his arm wildly at his brother.

"You can no hate hockey. You are, how you say, superstar?"

"And where did that get you, my brother?" Dmitri replied. The two brothers started shouting in Russian.

Tatiana looked more and more distraught. Finally, she stepped between the two, pushing them apart. "Enough, enough," she said fiercely. "You, Dmitri, you try to give us all something, but keep nothing for yourself."

She paused thoughtfully. "It is time for you now. If you say you so much hate hockey, then you must quit. Right now. We go back to Russia and I go back to teaching. Your choice. Not for me or Baba or Pavel. For you, now."

There was a moment of silence as Dmitri glowered at Tatiana. Then, slowly, a smile came across his face.

"You ask trick question," he said softly. "You know I can not give up hockey for good. For me, it is like breathing."

He shook his head. "I have forgotten so much. But when I play hockey with Gary on his rink, yes, that is really hockey. Next year, Pavel, you play hockey there with us too."

He took Tatiana in his arms and slapped Pavel playfully on the arm. His brother gave him an ear-to-ear grin.

"But I forget," Dmitri said, suddenly, his smile disappearing. "We will not be here next year."

"I stay here," Pavel said determinedly. "I will play on Gary's rink."

"But you might have no job when Snow Dogs go," his brother reminded him.

"What do you mean, Dmitri?" Gary asked.

"I stay here, work at rink. Even with no Snow Dogs, Socky say I have good job," Pavel insisted.

"What do you mean, 'no Snow Dogs'?" Gary persisted.

The Rushkovs exchanged guilty looks.

"It is secret," Tatiana explained gently. "The Snow Dogs, they will be going to someplace in United States. What is it called? Someplace hot."

"They're definitely going to move?" Gary exclaimed. "When did they decide this?"

"Pavel was at the arena today. They are moving all the Snow Dogs signs. He asked Socky. Socky say they move to United States," Tatiana explained. Pavel nodded vigorously.

"I think he is correct," Dmitri added sadly. "Darby say big announcement tomorrow. Darby is very angry."

"Dmitri, you've got to call my dad. Maybe there's some kind of legal thing he can do. We've got to try something," Gary pleaded.

Dmitri promised he would call. But Gary could tell by the expression on his friend's face that the Russian thought it was already too late.

MOVING OUT 27

GARY SPRINTED THE three blocks to the Civic Centre. As he got closer, he could see a large moving van parked alongside the arena. He raced around to the back door and almost crashed into Gunner.

The old trainer was carrying an armload of towels and jerseys. "Hey, watch where you're going!" he growled. Then his expression softened. "Oh, it's you, kid. Sorry. I thought it was another one of those souvenir hounds. They've been all over the place today, like a bunch of vultures picking over a carcass."

"What's going on?" Gary said, trying to catch his breath. He noticed a pile of Snow Dogs signs propped up against the wall. Wooden boxes lined the hallway.

"I guess you heard the news," Gunner said, dropping his pile into a large moving box.

"Pavel said the team is moving."

Gunner raised his eyebrows. "How are the Rushkovs? Dmitri was pretty shaken up the other night."

"He's okay, I guess. But he's upset the team is leaving."

Gunner sank down onto his bench. Gary noticed that his skate sharpener and tools were all gone. "It's just the way this business works, kid. They got a better offer. That's all it is. It's nothing against this town or anyone here. It's just a business."

"And you're going, too?"

"What else can I do? They're the only ones who'll keep an old coot like me around." Gunner scratched his head thoughtfully. "I don't know how many more of these moves I can take. I'm getting tired of always saying goodbye."

Dave Anderson came racing along the corridor. Gary noticed that the usually good-natured coach looked rattled. "Gunny, we've got to be out of here by noon at the latest," Anderson said sharply. He gave Gary a quick nod. "Dinsmore's holding a news conference and he wants us rolling out before he starts." Anderson rushed away down the hallway.

"I've got to get back to work, kid, or I'm going to be at it all night," the old trainer sighed heavily. "You take care. And you keep an eye on your Russian friends, alright?"

Gary nodded. The old trainer went back into the dressing room.

It was a miserable walk home. It had begun to rain in earnest now, and Gary was soaked to the skin by the time he got back to the house. He could hear his father shouting before he even opened the back door. He tried to sneak upstairs without his dad noticing, but Donny caught a glimpse of Gary out of the corner of his eye.

"Where have you been?" his father growled. "Never mind. I don't even care right now." Donny sank onto one of the stools along the kitchen counter. He stared for a moment at the cordless phone. He looked as if he was going to make another call and then shook his head. "The Snow Dogs are leaving, and there's nothing anyone can do about it."

"Dmitri already knows," Gary said.

Donny nodded. "I guess everyone figured it out when they started packing up gear. It's all but official now."

There was an awkward pause. "I'm sorry about the house," Donny said finally. "Maybe we should reconsider."

"No, you and Mom are right, I guess. It's just…"

"It's been a lot to go through in a short time."

Gary looked at his dad, surprised. Donny nodded. "I know. I feel that way too sometimes. And with everything that's been going on with Dmitri…we've had quite a winter."

"Yeah, quite a winter."

"But it wasn't all bad, Gary," his father said gently. "We've made some great new friends. And learned a little more than we wanted to about the business of hockey, I guess."

The game! How could he have forgotten? He quickly grabbed the cordless phone and dialled Todd's number.

"Alright!" he shouted as his friend told him the news. The Abbies had beaten Summerside 3–2 to tie the series at one win apiece. The next two games would be at the Civic Centre, on the Abbies' home turf.

"We really missed you," Todd added. "We're going to need a lot more goals to beat Summerside. Coach Mulligan wants to know if there's any way he can convince your dad to let you play."

"What about Justin?" Gary asked.

"Coach didn't say."

"I don't know, Todd. I'm just so tired of Justin getting his way all the time," Gary told his friend. "Besides, I'm not sure how much help I would be. My hand is pretty banged up."

"But it's the championship!" Todd urged him.

"I know. But when is Justin going to stop?"

"Well, he won't hurt you in the final. He knows that we need you back."

"At least he could apologize. Or admit that he slashed me."

"Yeah sure, Gary. That'll be when you-know-where freezes over," Todd said. His usually calm voice sounded angry.

"Todd, this isn't my fault," Gary argued.

"That's not what I meant," said Todd. "But I can't believe you're quitting on us."

Quitting? Gary was too angry to reply. "I'll see you at school," he said abruptly, slamming down the phone. He hadn't even had a chance to tell Todd that the Snow Dogs were leaving town tomorrow—for good.

BY MORNING, THE NEWS about the Snow Dogs had leaked out. Gary convinced Maggie to take him to the Civic Centre at lunch to watch Clark Dinsmore's news conference.

"I don't know why you're bothering," Maggie said sullenly. "What can he possibly say?"

"I just want to be there, okay?" They pulled into the crowded parking lot. Gary noticed that the moving van from last night was already gone.

Inside, a mob of fans and reporters crowded the lobby. A couple of fans wearing Snow Dogs jerseys had made signs: "Save our Snow Dogs," "Keep the Snow Dogs on PEI," and "Snow Dogs Stay!" There was a smattering of boos as Clark Dinsmore appeared on the makeshift stage. Gary almost crashed into Todd as he pushed through the crowd to get a better look. The two friends stood, side by side, though neither mentioned their fight the night before.

Dinsmore cleared his throat. "I just have a few brief comments and then I'll turn the microphone over to Dave Anderson and Darby Sanders, who will speak on behalf of the team. I would like to thank the people of Charlottetown and Prince Edward Island for their generosity and support over the last year. We are sorry we can't stay longer, but this is the reality of the hockey business today."

A couple of fans hissed, and Dinsmore gave them an angry glare as he stepped aside to let Darby Sanders speak. The team captain received a rousing cheer. He waved glumly from the podium. "I, too, want to thank the people of the Island for everything they've done to support this team. I also want to say a few words about my teammates, in particular, Dmitri Rushkov."

Gary elbowed Todd, and nodded in Dinsmore's direction. The president didn't look too pleased with his captain.

"Dmitri Rushkov is one of the finest people I've had the pleasure of playing with. I just wish it could have been longer. But Dmitri's talented, and he deserves to be playing in the NHL. He's going to be a major star someday." There was some half-hearted applause from the fans.

"No. You should clap harder than that," Sanders urged the crowd. "Don't believe what you've read in the papers. Dmitri has *always* been willing to play for this team. His not playing recently was the result of a management decision."

Now, all eyes were on Clark Dinsmore. He looked furious, and was gripping his notes, as if he'd like to clobber his player with them.

"Obviously, Mr. Dinsmore will not be happy with what I've said," Sanders continued, refusing to look over in the president's direction. "However, I feel I'm finally free to say how I feel. Places like Charlottetown deserve a hockey team. We've got to support Canadian hockey! And moving south of the border at the drop of a hat is no way to do that."

Dinsmore strode across the platform, but the crowd booed him and Darby Sanders waved him back. "One more thing. I am retiring from hockey. My family and I are returning to our hometown in New Brunswick. So, at least I'll be able to stay in the Maritimes. Thank you."

With that, Sanders waved to the crowd, climbed down the stairs of the stage, and headed toward the door. A clutch of cameras and reporters followed him.

A shaken Dave Anderson took his place at the podium. "I don't think there's much left for me to say. Darby has, as usual, said it all." He gave a half-hearted grin. Then his face grew dark. "I, too, regret what has happened. But I'm even more upset about the way Dmitri has been treated. He's just a kid, far from home. We sometimes forget that. And above all, we need to remember that hockey is just a game. Just a game—but the greatest game on earth."

The Coach's words were thick with emotion and he nervously wiped his face. "I will always remember my time here." The tears welled up in his eyes as he moved away from the podium.

Dinsmore waved to the crowd. "That's it. Show's over." The hockey executive turned and jumped off the back of the stage, disappearing down one of the hallways before the media could catch him.

ONE LAST CHANCE 28

"WHAT A SLIMEBALL!" Todd exclaimed as Clark Dinsmore disappeared and the crowd started to break up, still grumbling. Gary jumped as he felt a hand on his shoulder.

"Take care, kid." It was Dave Anderson. "Maybe we'll meet again someday. Keep working on that backhand." With a wink, Anderson disappeared after his boss.

"Cool!" Todd said, slapping his friend on the arm. "Dave Anderson thinks you're good." Gary felt himself blushing. "He forgot to mention that I need to grow. Like, a lot!"

The boys headed toward the door. Suddenly, Todd stopped. "Wait." He turned to stand back-to-back with Gary, and then put his hand on top of both of their heads.

"Hey, I thought so!" Todd turned to face Gary again. "You keep whining about not growing, but you're almost as tall as me now."

Gary gave his friend a nudge. "Okay, catching up to the big guy!" They walked out of the rink laughing. Maggie waved to them from the parked minivan.

"What's so funny?" she said sarcastically. "What I heard on the radio didn't make me laugh."

"Oh, it's just that Dave Anderson said I was good. And then Todd was forced to admit that I was probably better than him," Gary teased. He gave his friend a playful shot in the shoulder, and Todd gave one right back. Maggie rolled her eyes.

"What else did they say on the radio?" Gary asked. Maggie manoeuvred the minivan out onto the street.

"Well, all of a sudden Dmitri's a big hero again. And Darby's speech blew everyone away. The radio guys said if more people thought like him, we wouldn't keep losing teams in places like Charlottetown."

"Well, now *we* have to focus on winning the championship," Todd said.

"Maybe Dmitri can play for the Abbies," Maggie teased.

Her brother gave her a dirty look. "I just wish *I* could."

"SO HOW IS YOUR HAND?" Todd asked later that afternoon. They were walking through the hallway between classes.

"It's still not great. I guess it doesn't really matter what my dad says. I wouldn't be able to play much anyway."

"Game three isn't until tomorrow night! I'm sure your hand will be better by then. Can't you work on your dad?" Todd urged.

"I am!"

"So you *do* want to play?"

Gary stopped and stared at his friend. "I *always* wanted to play. I would never let my team down."

"Oh, really?" Todd raised his eyebrows. "Are you sure about that? Sometimes it seems like you're too busy feeling sorry for yourself to even think about the team."

Gary glared furiously at his friend before storming down the hall.

That evening, Gary stared out his window at the melting ice of the backyard rink, glimmering in the moonlight. He mulled over his friend's statement. Had he let his team down? He thought back to earlier in the year, when it looked like the Coach was going to send him down to AA. Back then, all that mattered was playing for the Abbies. What had changed? He stared down at the rink but for once, The Dream wouldn't come.

THE ABBIES WON GAME three on Thursday night. Gary spent a miserable evening moping around the house, dreading going to school the next day. He even thought about pretending he was sick so he wouldn't have to face his teammates. Obviously, the Abbies were fine without him. One more win and the series was over.

Before he left, Gary wrapped his hand in the tensor bandage, even though he had been fine without it the night before. When he ran into Todd in the hall, the two boys nodded at each other, but didn't say a word. At lunch, Todd sat with the Abbies, while Gary ate alone.

The school had organized a pep rally for the last ten minutes of Friday afternoon. While his class made its way down the hall to the gym, Gary slipped into the bathroom and ducked inside a stall. He could hear the music and cheering in the distance. This is a new low, he thought. When the hallway was clear, he snuck out a side door into the spring sunshine. Almost all the snow had melted. Hockey season was over.

BY SUNDAY AFTERNOON, a permanent lump had lodged in Gary's stomach. The Abbies had lost the game Saturday night at the Civic Centre, 3–2. Now, the championship was down to the fifth and deciding game—a game that would be played in Summerside, in front of all their raucous fans. Gary worried that the Abbies would be outmatched by the sheer force of the Summerside cheering section.

As the day wore on he grew more and more anxious. He thought about how tired his teammates must be after the roller-coaster ride of the series. At four o'clock, he looked anxiously out the window. Todd would be eating now and then leaving for the hour-long drive to Summerside. Gary felt the lump in his stomach growing. It was the last game of the season. He slowly unwrapped the tensor bandage and wiggled his fingers. His hand was fine. He knew what he had to do.

TEAMMATES—FOR REAL 29

HALF AN HOUR LATER, his mother honked the horn from his driveway. Gary was waiting anxiously by the door, his hockey bag in hand.

"Where's your dad?" his mom asked. "I thought he'd want to take you to the game. After all, he was the one who insisted on that other boy being kicked off the team."

"He and Lisa had something they needed to do," Gary replied cryptically. He hoped his mother wouldn't ask too many more questions.

As they cruised along the highway to Summerside, Gary distracted his mother with small talk. He told her about Pavel's job at the Civic Centre and filled her in about Dmitri and Tatiana's wedding plans. "It's going to be here on the Island and we're all invited," Gary said, genuinely enthusiastic. Then he remembered where they were headed and his stomach lurched again.

"It sounds like a happy ending for everyone!" his mother exclaimed.

Gary frowned. "Except for the Snow Dogs leaving."

"I was shocked to hear they were going," his mother agreed. "I'm in business, too, and I don't think my company would do very well if it kept picking up and leaving town every year or so. That's just bad management."

"I guess hockey is different," Gary replied.

"Well, they claim that it's about business. I think what they mean is that it's about making money, no matter what the cost to the players and the community." Gary was surprised to hear his mother speak so passionately. He didn't think she had really paid all that much attention to the Snow Dogs.

"I'm sure another team will come here someday," Gary suggested.

His mother gave him a sharp look. "Do you really think so? I think the future of professional hockey is those big arenas in the southern United States. That's where the sport is headed now. Little hockey communities like ours don't seem to count for much in the bigger scheme of things."

Gary knew his mother was right. He looked out the window and wiggled his fingers, trying to warm them up for the game. All of a sudden, a winter's worth of memories came rushing back—his concussion, meeting Dmitri, watching Socky living out his former hockey glory, Christmas at his mom's new apartment.

He thought about all the changes his family had been through, and he realized that, in a way, things had worked out. Not exactly as he thought they would, but his life was okay.

"Thanks for giving me a ride," he said, turning to his mother. He wanted to say much more—about how rotten he had been to her all winter, and about how sorry he was—but he just couldn't find the words. He looked out the window again.

"That's okay," his mother said gently, as if she somehow knew what he was thinking. "We're almost there. You'd better start thinking about the game."

GARY HAD BUTTERFLIES in his stomach as he and his mother walked into the stadium. "See you after the game," his mother said. She gave him a reassuring smile as he disappeared down the hallway toward the dressing rooms.

Gary swung the door of the locker room open. The music was blaring and everyone was already starting to get changed. His teammates looked surprised to see him, but no one said a word. Justin turned away quickly, and kept on getting dressed. Gary put his bag and stick down next to Todd's locker.

"It's so cool that you're going to play," Todd whispered. "And that your dad finally gave in."

"Uh, yeah," Gary said, looking down at his hockey bag to hide his confusion. How did Todd know? Had his mom called the Coach before they left Charlottetown?

"What's up in here?" Gary asked Todd. "Why's everybody so quiet?"

"Mulligan's off having some big shouting match with Justin's dad. The Coach wants to kick him out of the game because of what he did to you. Justin's freaking because he wants to play."

Gary glanced over to the other end of the dressing room where the older boy was lacing up his skates. He had never seen Justin looking so serious.

"Why did the Coach change his mind?" Gary asked softly.

"When he heard you were coming, he told Justin that the team needed you more than we needed him," Todd answered, sneaking a look in Justin's direction. "Justin knows that you're better than him. That's why he's been on your case all year."

For the first time, Gary felt sorry for the older player. He tried to put himself in Justin's shoes. Until Gary and Todd showed up, Justin had been the star of the team. These days, he was being overshadowed by two younger players. And he and Todd were almost as big as Justin now. If Justin had finished his growth spurt, he would no longer be able to rely on bullying everyone to get his way.

Suddenly, the door swung open. Russ looked around the locker room. "MacDonald. Johnston. Come with me."

Russ led the two boys down the hallway to the medical room. Coach Mulligan was sitting there with Justin's dad. The Coach chewed thoughtfully on his cigar. "Gary, I need you to sort something out for me. Mr. Johnston here doesn't believe that his dear little Justin slashed you. I'd like you to explain what happened, so that I can kick this troublemaker off the team once and for all."

Gary squirmed uncomfortably under Mr. Johnston's icy gaze. He could feel Justin beside him, though he was too scared to make eye contact. Gary looked desperately at his coach, hoping for some guidance. Mulligan gestured for him to begin.

"It was, uh, after the game. After he missed the goal," Gary began.

"It was a lousy pass!" Mr. Johnston butted in.

"One more word and he's out!" Mulligan shouted. "MacDonald, continue."

"I, uh, slipped..."

"The truth, MacDonald."

Gary took a deep breath. "Yeah, he slashed me. But he was frustrated. We'd just lost the game. But I don't want him to miss *this* game. We need everyone, Coach," Gary pleaded.

Mulligan looked perplexed. "I can't let him get away with slashing his own player, Gary."

"But, Coach, it's the championship," Gary urged. "Let him play. This is our last chance. And my hand is fine. That's what's important." Gary looked over at the older player. He was white as a ghost.

"No, that's *not* what's important. Doing what's right is important," Mulligan argued. "Your father was right. I was wrong."

"I never thought I'd hear those words." Gary was shocked to hear his father's voice outside the door. "May I come in? The door was open."

"Oh, now he gets into the act, too," Mr. Johnston sneered.

Coach Mulligan threw his cigar to the ground. "That's it. Get him outta here!"

Donny raised his hands. "Wait a minute, guys. Let's calm down and think this through."

Mr. Johnston nodded slightly. "Sorry, I just got a little carried away."

"Yeah, and so did your kid. He almost broke my son's hand," Donny continued. "Gary has had everything going against him this season, including your son. But he stuck it out through the head injuries, getting back in shape, and being put on the fourth line. Then Justin almost ruins it all."

"C'mon, your kid has talent to spare," Mr. Johnston said. "Justin's the one who's taken a beating this season." The two dads glared at each other.

"We're getting nowhere with this," the Coach intervened. "We've got half an hour to game time. I've got to make a decision." He turned to Gary. "Kid, it's up to you."

Gary looked at his dad, then at Justin. Then he turned to the Coach. "I think Justin should play."

"Alright. You two, back to the dressing room," Mulligan clapped his hands together. "And not a word to the rest of the boys."

Gary and Justin started back to the dressing room. Gary could hear the music pounding away in the stadium and the sound of the crowd making their way through the stands.

"Gary!" his father shouted, just as he reached the locker room door. He stopped, moving aside to let Justin past. "Thanks," Justin mumbled as he went through the door.

"I'm sorry, Dad," Gary turned to his father. "I didn't mean to lie to Mom, but I just had to be here. And my hand is fine."

"It's okay, Gary." Donny motioned for his son to be quiet. "I was wrong. It should have been your choice all along. It was just hard for me to sit back and watch that boy hurt you."

"So, I can play?" Gary asked anxiously. His father nodded. He gave Gary a quick bear hug. "Oh, and by the way, Dmitri, Pavel, and Tatiana are here for the game. I thought you'd like to know."

"Thanks, Dad," Gary smiled. Then, his hand on the door to the dressing room, he turned back to where his father was standing. "How did you know I was here? And to bring them to the game?"

"Your mother was worried about your hand and called me on my cell. I guess I realized then how determined you were to play. So I called the Coach to tell him you were coming and then stopped by the Rushkovs to invite them along. Maggie's here too and she says to tell you she told you so."

Gary laughed. He'd almost forgotten! When the season had started, he didn't even think he'd make the Abbies— never mind play on the first line in the championship game. His sister had been right, after all.

"But, Gary. One more thing." His father paused, and his face went stern. "Don't *ever* pull a stunt like this on me again!"

Gary was relieved to see his father chuckling as the door to the locker room swung shut.

30 FINALLY, THE CHAMPIONSHIP!

THE CHAMPIONSHIP GAME was a spirited match. The teams were evenly matched, and it quickly became obvious that neither side was going to make it easy for the other. By the end of two periods, the game was tied two-all. Todd and Gary each had a goal and Justin had already served two penalties for fighting. He hadn't said another word to Gary and avoided going anywhere near him when they were on the ice.

"This is it, boys." Coach Mulligan rallied his troops before heading out for the third period. "It doesn't get much better than this. Let's do it."

The Coach juggled the lineup again and replaced Justin on the first line. Gary sensed the older boy growing more and more frustrated. On his next shift, Justin tried to slash the other team's top forward. The referee took him to the penalty box again. Coach Mulligan shook his head in disgust. "Great. Another power play for them. What's wrong with that kid?"

Russ tapped Gary and Todd on their shoulders. He was sending them out to kill off the penalty. "Heads up, boys," he warned them. "Their enforcer may try for some payback."

As they lined up for the faceoff, Gary noticed a large Summerside player looking over at him. The player gave Gary a surly nod. Then he turned his attention to Todd. "Watch out, Todd!" Gary whispered to his friend. As soon as the ref dropped the puck, the tough guy made a run at Todd and pushed him into the boards. Gary missed the rest of what happened as the action moved down the ice. He turned back when the whistle blew and noticed his friend crumpled on the ice.

"It's my shoulder," Todd winced as Gary skated over. "It feels just like the last time." The arena's medical staff came running out with a stretcher and pushed Gary aside. He skated, shaken, back to the bench.

"It's his shoulder," he told Coach Mulligan, who slapped his forehead and groaned. "Go tell Johnston that he's on your line again when he's out of the box," Mulligan shouted at Gary, who reluctantly skated over to the penalty box.

"You're on my line," he muttered to Justin.

"Whatever, MacWuss. It's not as if we have a chance of winning this game anyway," Justin grumbled.

Just then, Doug Currie skated up to the box. "We'd already have the championship if you would stop taking stupid penalties," he said as he pulled Gary away.

Gary was astonished. Doug was one of Justin's friends! "Forget him," Doug said. "Change of plans. I'm up on your line now. Hope that's cool."

"Yeah, sure," Gary said, still a little unsure of what was going on. He looked over at Justin who was trying to shout something at the referee.

"What an idiot!" Doug rolled his eyes. "Man, it's hard to concentrate when he's being such a jerk. I think the Coach is going to bench him now. We can't risk any more stupid penalties."

Gary skated a few loops around the zone as the attendants finished carrying Todd off the ice. He looked up in the stands where his parents, Maggie, and the Rushkovs were sitting. "He's okay," he mouthed, giving them a thumbs-up. Dmitri gave him a thumbs-up back and Tatiana and Pavel waved.

Gary took his place at the faceoff circle. There were still five minutes left in the game. They didn't want to go into overtime, especially now that Todd was out. The Abbies needed to win this game soon.

Gary won the faceoff and passed the puck to Doug. He fumbled it and Summerside took over, skating down the ice. It was a pattern that repeated itself again and again over the next four minutes. The Abbies would gain some ground and Doug would fall behind.

On the bench between shifts Gary ended up next to Justin, who had just come out of the penalty box. Gary refused to make eye contact and Justin didn't seem to notice. He was too busy shouting obscenities at the Summerside players as they went past.

It was down to the final minute of play. Russ tapped on Gary's shoulder and pointed to the ice. "You're up next." Justin started to get up, too. "Don't bother," Russ said coolly. "Currie's still on the first line."

"But he sucks. Are you watching the same game? He totally messed up his last two shifts," Justin scowled.

"I don't care," Coach Mulligan said, coming over to sort out the confusion. "Currie's my pick. Got it?"

As they took their places, Gary gave Doug an encouraging look. "Don't worry about him. Like you said, he's a jerk. Just keep it simple." Doug nodded.

Gary won the faceoff and proceeded down the ice. It was almost the identical play to last weekend, when Justin had missed the net. Again, the Summerside players made their move on Gary. He hesitated for a moment. Should he take the shot himself this time? He deked past one of the players and made his move toward the net. Just as the Summerside defenceman put out his stick, Gary slid the puck over to Doug. The goalie had already repositioned himself to stop Gary. He had no time to get back across the open mouth of the net. Doug tapped the puck slightly and it dribbled, slowly, across the line.

The Abbies' bench erupted and everyone poured out onto the ice. Gary finally broke away and took a look up at the clock. There were still ten seconds left! "Guys, guys! It's not over yet. Get back on the bench." He looked over anxiously at the referee. He'd been called over to the Summerside bench where the coaching staff was pointing wildly at the scoreboard.

"Get off the ice! Get off the ice! We're going to get a penalty!" Russ and the other coaches were trying to get the Abbies back on the bench, while Coach Mulligan was waving the referee over to his side. But it was too late.

"Too many men on the ice," the referee called. "One of you, in the box. Now." He grabbed Gary and pulled him over to the penalty box.

Gary stood anxiously as the two teams lined up. He was surprised to see Justin taking the faceoff. What was the Coach trying to do?

The linesman dropped the puck. Justin won the faceoff and quickly dumped the puck out of the Abbies' zone. The

Summerside goalie flipped it in the air and down the length of the ice. Gary held his breath as the puck landed. One of the Summerside players took a shot, just as Justin threw himself in front of the puck. The buzzer went and once again, the Abbies started to celebrate. Gary raced out of the box toward the crowd of players. He noticed Justin hunched over by the glass. There was blood streaming down his face. One of the trainers raced over with a towel.

"I guess I got in front of that last shot," Justin said as the trainer tilted his head back. "What a way to end the season."

"Great shift, Johnston," Gary tapped Justin on the arm. "You did good."

The older player gave a rueful smile. "Coming from you, MacWuss, that means a lot." He got up slowly and skated over to the bench while Gary joined the rest of his teammates at centre ice.

Because Todd couldn't lift the trophy, Gary accepted the championship cup. He skated over to where his friend was standing and let him kiss the trophy. Then Gary took the cup and put it above his head. He skated triumphantly past the stands, where his family and the Russians were standing. He could see Dmitri pumping his arm in the air. Gary handed the cup over to Justin, who was next in line.

"No hard feelings, MacWuss," Justin said, grabbing the trophy. Gary just smiled. Not even Justin could spoil this moment.

THE RINK 31

GARY DROVE HOME in the minivan with Dmitri, Pavel, and Tatiana. Along the way, they eagerly relived every moment of the exciting final game.

"Your season ends much better than mine," said Dmitri, only half teasing. He was right. The New Mexico Snow Dogs had just barely missed the playoffs. And because Dmitri had missed so many games, he had lost any chance of the rookie-of-the-year award. Still, the Russian was hopeful about next season. The Snow Dogs had renegotiated his contract, and Dmitri, Tatiana, and Baba would be moving to New Mexico in September.

Only Pavel was staying on in Prince Edward Island. His leg was healing well, and Darby Sanders had invited him to Moncton for a couple of weeks over the summer to help run a hockey camp for kids. And he was going to continue his job at the Civic Centre.

"I will miss your hockey rink next season," Dmitri said as they drew closer to Charlottetown. "They no have such rinks in New Mexico."

"No, but you could have a roller skating rink in your back-yard!" Gary teased.

Gary knew how much he was going to miss Dmitri. The Russian player had certainly helped him through some tough times, and Gary knew that he'd been a good friend to Dmitri as well. He could hardly believe that he'd never go to another Snow Dogs game in Charlottetown again. The realization made him sad. But it would be good to have Pavel around, and they'd all be able to watch Dmitri on television playing for New Mexico.

After they dropped their Russian friends off, Gary and his dad drove home in a contented silence. As they pulled into the driveway, Donny stopped for a moment with the engine idling. The lights of the minivan shone on the empty boards of the ice rink, which was now almost totally melted.

"I'm going to miss this place," Donny said, his voice filled with emotion.

For just a moment, they both stared at the watery oval, as if they could see the ghosts of past games streaking up and down the glistening ice. Then Donny turned off the lights, and the ghosts disappeared.

"Maybe the next family will have a couple of kids, too," Donny suggested, pulling his son's hockey gear out of the van and slinging it over his shoulder.

"That would be good." Gary replied. And he meant it.